LOVE AND DEFECTS

A HOCKEY FRIENDS TO LOVERS ROMANCE

PERFECTLY IMPERFECT SERIES

WEST GREENE

Copyright ©August 2023 by West Greene

All rights reserved.

No part of this book may be reproduced in any form or by any electronic or mechanical means, including information storage and retrieval systems, without written permission from the author, except for the use of brief quotations in a book review.

Formatting: Tiff Writes Romance

Cover Design: Tiff Writes Romance

Editing: Tiff Writes Romance

Proofreading: Kimberly Peterson

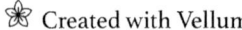 Created with Vellum

For Riley, my reason for everything that I do.

For every person healing from trauma, please know you're not alone. Every storm creates a beautiful rainbow.

BOOKS IN THIS SERIES:

My Contributions:
All His Broken Pieces
Love and Defects

NOTE FROM THE AUTHOR:

This book contains situations and elements that some readers may not find enjoyable. These include PTSD, flashbacks, child abuse, sexual assault, rape, erectile dysfunction (ED), and bullying.

If you find any of the above triggering, I advise against reading.

If you have any questions, please feel free to reach out to me via email at author westgreene@gmail.com

PROLOGUE

Sterling

Darren ran his palms up my chest, and I swallowed back vile, his touch making my skin clammy. For two months now, Darren had been pushing me for more. But I hadn't been ready. Honestly, I still wasn't. It wasn't easy for me to allow people I didn't feel one hundred percent safe with to touch me. It made my skin crawl.

Nausea swirled in my gut, and I squeezed my eyes shut when *his* voice taunted in my ear, *"That's right, pretty boy. I'm the only one who gets to touch you."*

"Stop," I blurted, all of the muscles in my body locking up. Both of us were naked by that point, and even though Darren was gorgeous as hell with thick muscles and abs I'd once daydreamed about licking, I couldn't do this. I was ready to tear my skin off with my nails just so I couldn't feel him touching me anymore. And I wasn't hard. Not in the slightest.

It'd been a problem for me for as long as I could remember, but I didn't know how to bring it up to anyone, not even a doctor. I sure as hell couldn't bring it up to my parents. Puberty hit, and my dick barely did anything. And that still hadn't changed over the years. I managed to get hard for a second, but then *he* would flash into my head, and I would go soft. And if someone was touching me that I didn't feel safe with, it was like my dick wanted to get sucked into my body.

One would think after being rescued fifteen years ago from that crazed predator, I'd be over this. But some things stuck with you. And for me, this was one of those things.

Being sexually abused by my father for *years* had fucked me up in so many ways, I lost track of them all. Hell, I *still* came across shit that triggered the hell out of me. It was a never-ending cycle of destruction that I couldn't escape.

"You've got to be fucking kidding me," Darren snarled, shoving away from me. He picked up my limp dick, and I bit my tongue hard enough to draw blood to beat back my fear at his unwanted touch. "You're not even fucking hard. You got a goddamn problem, Sterling? This isn't the first time I've noticed you can't get your dick up."

I flinched, pain slicing through my chest from his harsh words. It didn't matter that he and I weren't really invested in each other. Words still cut me deeply.

Sue me, I was a fucking softie. And I took everything to heart.

"Fuck you," I muttered, rolling off my bed. I snatched a pair of sweats off the floor. Pretty sure they were Graham's—my roommate and best friend—and they were probably dirty, but oh, well. They'd do. I *needed* to cover up before I tried shedding my fucking skin. "Get the hell out, Darren."

"Fucking gladly," he snarled. He got off the bed and yanked his jeans off the floor. "And this—" he snapped, gesturing between us once his jeans were zipped, "is fucking over. Lose my goddamn number until you learn how to get your dick up."

Not even bothering to pull on his shirt or his shoes, he stormed out of the dorm room, slamming the door shut behind him so hard, the sound rattled my teeth.

I blew out a soft breath and focused on my shoes as I waited for Dr. Clancy, my therapist, to call me back for my two-thirty appointment with her. I was missing class for this, but I *needed* to see her. And two-thirty was the only slot she had available today.

I'd barely slept last night. Having Darren touch me had awoken a whole bunch of shit I wasn't prepared to face. I shouldn't have pushed myself to have sex before I was ready. Before I fully trusted Darren. I mean, fuck, it'd taken me almost an entire year to be comfortable enough with Graham touching me. Why did I think I'd be able to let Darren touch me like that after only knowing each other for three months?

"Sterling?" I heard Dr. Clancy call, snatching me out of my head. I glanced up and forced myself to my feet when I saw her standing at the door, holding it open for me. She smiled at me, but there was concern etched into her eyes. "How are you, hun?"

"Been better," I muttered. And that was as close to the truth as I was willing to spew when people could hear.

I'd been seeing Dr. Clancy since I was a kid and my parents adopted me. They'd searched everywhere for the best trauma therapist for me, not caring what kind of distance they needed to drive. So, when I was choosing a college, this one was a no-brainer for me. Her office was within walking distance of campus, which was useful because I *hated* driving.

We walked down the hall and entered her cozy office. It was done in dark brown and deep burgundy colors, and black-out drapes covered her windows. Her dark office had always helped soothe me when talking about things. My father had always kept me in well-lit rooms so he could see all of me. So, I sought comfort in the darkness.

"What's going on, Sterling? It's not like you to call and make an appointment outside of our normal times."

I blew out a soft breath and sat on the couch across from her comfy-looking chair. Rubbing my hands together, I leaned forward, chewing on my bottom lip. "Last night, I tried to have sex with the guy I've been seeing for the last couple of months. It, um... It didn't go well."

She nodded with no hint of judgment in her facial expression. "Tell me about it."

I leaned back and sort of wrapped my arms around myself as a chill swept through my body. "I heard *his* voice in my head," I rasped. "He called me pretty boy." Another chill raced down my spine, and goosebumps popped up on my flesh. I rubbed my arms as if a cool breeze had blown over my body. "I told Darren to stop, and then he made everything worse when he touched me. Grabbed my dick," I explained. She didn't even flinch at my crass language. I was sure there wasn't much she hadn't heard in all her years of being a therapist. "He was giving me hell for my dick always being soft."

"That's a lot to unpack," Dr. Clancy began. I nodded in agreement. I knew it was, which was why I was here. I wasn't afraid to seek help when I could sense I was spiraling. "First, let's start with you being soft, even when you should be sexually aroused. How long has that been happening?"

I flushed. I hadn't expected her to zero in on that so fast. "Um... always?" I said, though it came out as more of a question. "I haven't ever been able to keep an erection."

"You haven't told anyone before today, have you?" she asked me. I could hear the disapproving note in her voice. When I shook my head, she sighed. "Before you leave today, I'll refer you to a doctor I trust. He's been in the business a long time."

I sighed, hating it was coming to this, but she was right. I needed to see a specialist. I couldn't keep ignoring this. "What do you think is wrong with me?" I asked her.

"I believe you have erectile dysfunction," she gently explained. I blew out a soft breath. Fucking great. "But I believe it's linked to your trauma and PTSD. But I want a second opinion before I do anything further."

"Okay," I said quietly, leaving it at that. I trusted Dr. Clancy to help me make the best decisions for my body. And God, it would be nice to one day be able to be on the receiving end of sex rather than always being the giver. I didn't *mind* being the giver —loved it actually. But I'd like to receive the same in return.

"Can I ask why you felt the need to have sex with Darren, and you haven't known him long?" she asked me next, sensing I wanted to move on from the topic as well. I'd told her the moment I decided to give Darren a chance. She'd encouraged me but also reminded me to be cautious.

I'd obviously thrown caution out the window last night.

"He's been pushing for it," I told her. "I mean, I'm fine giving oral sex. That doesn't bother me. But every time he touched me, I clammed up. And I should've known I wasn't ready, but I thought I could just get through it."

She leaned forward a little, her eyes meeting my dark ones. "Sterling, trauma is not something you just *get through*. What you endured and the memories you have to live with should not be taken lightly. It doesn't matter that it happened fifteen years ago. You have to do what you're comfortable with and what doesn't trigger you."

"And being touched by people I don't trust is a trigger," I muttered.

She nodded. "We both know it is, hun. Stop being so hard on yourself. Stop pushing yourself to do things you know won't work out in the end just because you think they *should*. These memories will be there for the rest of your life, and the trauma, the triggers, the anxiety—it's all going to follow."

"I know," I grunted. I just wanted to be *normal*.

She reached across the small distance between us, and after I nodded at her, she gently squeezed my knee. She was one of the few people I trusted to touch me, but when I was feeling out of sorts like I was right now, she knew she needed to ask for permission.

Everyone close to me did.

"You're going to find someone one day who makes you happy and makes you feel safe," she assured me. "But don't force it." Then, she grabbed her laptop and opened it up. "Let me write up this referral and print it out for you. I want you to go see this doctor as soon as possible, okay?"

I nodded. "Got it."

She smiled at me. "This is just a tiny setback, Sterling. It's not the end of the world. So, take a deep breath, file this away in your trigger file, and be aware that being touched sexually by someone you're not comfortable with brings *him* forth, okay?"

Oh, trust—I did that last night the second it happened.

But still, I just said, "I will."

I blew out a soft breath as I laid back on the cot in the ultrasound room I was in. From what I understood, some weird wand-looking thing called a transducer was going to be used to get images of my blood vessels to check the blood flow to my dick. I'd requested a woman to do it, and while the nurse had looked a little weirded out, the doctor had agreed and told me he'd stand in the room but nowhere near me.

Thank God for accommodating and understanding doctors.

"Just breathe," the lady told me. "I don't have any reason to touch you like you're worried about."

"Sorry," I mumbled. I drew in a deep breath. "Touch is triggering for me."

She nodded in understanding. "We're

going to take good care of you here," she promised me. "And I'll make this as quick as possible."

"Okay." I drew in another deep breath and slowly released it before shutting my eyes and nodding for her to go ahead. A few minutes later, it was all over and I was dressed back in my normal clothes, waiting for the results of all the exams, blood work, and the ultrasound.

My phone buzzed in my hand as I chilled on the cot, and I looked down at it, clicking on Graham's text.

> Graham: Hey, just came in from class to grab lunch with you. Where are you?

I cringed. I hadn't told him what was going on, and I knew he was worried about me because I wasn't being my normal self with him. I was just struggling and needed time. Graham was good about giving me that, but it didn't mean he wouldn't hover.

> Sterling: I had to take care of something. Have lunch without me. I'll grab something on my way back to campus.

> Graham: Promise?

I smiled a little. God, I was so in love with my best friend, it was sickening to even think about. Ever since Graham met me at the beginning of freshman year, he went out of his way to learn everything he could to help me. I struggled to eat on my bad days, so he found things that were easy for me to keep down like soup, crackers, broth, and scrambled eggs of all things. When he would find me gone in the middle of the night to go running to burn off steam and nervous energy—and to try running away from my thoughts—he would come hunt me down and just fall into step beside me without ever saying a word.

Graham had become my lifeline. He hadn't batted an eye when he found out I couldn't stand being touched by people I didn't know, so the entire first year we were living together, he worked with me to gain my trust. But he also let me touch him first. It took months for me to allow him to touch me, but I swore I saw tears in his eyes when I finally did.

> Sterling: Promise. I'll even send a pic of what I order.

> Graham: I'm holding you to that.

I snickered and then locked my screen when a light knock sounded on the door. The doctor walked in and took a seat on his stool. "There's nothing wrong," he told me. "Physically, there are no blockages. All of your vitals are great. Your bloodwork came back perfect, and I didn't find anything on your physical or your ultrasound. I believe Dr. Clancy is right, and you're suffering a mental block."

I sighed, my shoulders slumping. If that was the case, then there was no hope for me. We'd tried multiple medications, but I always had horrible side effects from them, so I eventually just stopped trying medications altogether when I was seventeen. My parents hadn't liked it, nor had Dr. Clancy, but everyone had supported me.

"Thanks, doc."

He nodded. "I wish there was more I could do for you, Sterling. I really do. I think this is something you and Dr. Clancy need to work through together."

I slid off the cot. "Thanks, doc," I repeated, just wanting this day over with. "I'll talk to her about it at my next appointment. Will everything be faxed over to her?"

He nodded. "I've got someone working on it as we speak," he assured me. "You have a good day, Sterling."

"You, too," I muttered before I walked out of the room, heading to the checkout counter.

1

Graham

Something was wrong with Sterling. This was the third morning in a row he had slipped out of our dorm in his running clothes. He was doing his best to hide his spiraling from me, but hell, we were into our third year of friendship. I knew Sterling like the back of my hand.

Something had happened. Even Darren had been pissy at practice the last couple of days. In fact, it'd been since Sterling had asked me if he could have the dorm to himself for the night. Fuck, that had settled in my stomach like sour ass milk when he requested it, but I'd done it. I'd shoved aside my own feelings so Sterling could have the opportunity to get off with a guy that wasn't me.

I'd holed up with a girl a couple of floors beneath us. It was easier than trying to room with another guy on our floor, who would probably have their own conquests in their beds.

The girl I'd stayed with—I couldn't even remember her damn name—had tried to have sex with me, but I hadn't been in the mood. All I could think about was my best friend—the guy I was madly in love with—being upstairs with one of my jackass teammates.

Hell, anyone who wasn't me was a jackass when it came to Sterling. No one was good enough for him. Because despite everything he'd been through, he still had a heart of gold and a soul that just shone a light on anyone who needed it.

He was everything good in this world.

And I was terrified someone would be able to snuff it out if I didn't protect him.

Clenching my jaw, I slid out of bed and grabbed my toiletries. I knew Sterling would be gone for a good minute, so I had time to shower and get dressed for the day before confronting him. And I *would* be confronting him because he and I both knew that nothing good ever came out of him trying to outrun his demons.

It just left him exhausted. It didn't fix him not being able to sleep. It didn't fix whatever was happening in his life to keep him wired, anxious, and worried.

The trauma Sterling had endured... God, it made me sick to my stomach to even think about it. He hadn't told me everything. Hell, I was pretty sure he'd barely even scraped the surface of what he'd gone through and what that sick son of a bitch had done to him when he'd talked to me about it. But he'd told me enough for me to know it was fucking horrendous.

Most people wouldn't be able to live with those kinds of memories haunting them day in and day out. I wasn't sure I could. Sterling was the strongest person I knew. I just wished he saw that so he didn't spend so much time running from the darkness in his mind.

Grunting, I stood in front of the mirror and began to shave my face. I hated having any kind of stubble. Didn't know why, but it bothered the fuck out of me. I loved stubble and beards on other men. Loved the way it felt against my skin. But I hated my own stubble. I'd even tried growing it out once to see if that made it any better, but nope. Hated it even more.

Besides, Sterling didn't seem to mind my face being free of hair every day.

After shaving, I quickly got in the shower, knowing I didn't have much more time before Sterling made it back to the dorms. In five minutes, I was out, dried off, and dressed, heading back into our room. Sterling was rifling through his little closet for clothes, and he turned to look at me when I entered.

His back tensed when I flipped the lock.

I hated making him feel trapped, but if I didn't, he'd run.

Again.

"We need to talk," I told him as I ran my towel over my wet, dirty blonde hair.

He grunted. "Nothing to talk about, Graham."

I snorted and dropped onto my bed. "Cut the bullshit, Sterling. I know you well enough to know something's wrong. Not only have you gone for a run the past two days and again this morning, but you're eating less, and you're hardly sleeping."

He hung his head forward, his shoulders slumping. I hated the defeat so clearly riding him. My fingers twitched with the urge to tug him into my arms, but I wasn't sure what mood he was in right now. Touching him in the wrong mood could send him falling into a panic attack. And fuck, those were terrifying to witness.

I *hated* it when he had panic attacks. They made me feel hopeless. Useless. And I felt like I was suffocating right along with him.

"Come on, Sterling," I pleaded. "I'm worried about you."

He clenched his jaw before looking at me. "I really don't want to talk about it, Graham."

"Tough," I bit back at him, matching his grumpy attitude with my own. "Neither of us is leaving this room until you open your mouth and tell me what the hell is going on with you."

He snorted. "I'd like to see you try to stop me," he retorted.

I arched a brow at him, crossing my arms over my chest. I was slim, just like him, but I had more muscle mass from playing hockey and all the practice and weight training I had to endure day after day. "Wanna test me?" I taunted.

He growled something under his breath I couldn't catch, but he slunk to his bed before plopping down on it. His skin was still slightly glistening from his run, and it made me want to push him back on his mattress, straddle his hips, and lick all that salty sweat off of his skin.

And fuck—my dick was hard.

"It's embarrassing," Sterling finally said, staring at the floor between his feet. His leg began to bounce, a nervous tick he had. I wanted to grip his thigh and soothe him, my fingers twitching with the need, but I held myself back.

"Sterling, nothing you say to me could ever be embarrassing, especially if it's bothering you." And I meant that. "Just talk to me. Because I'm going nuts with worry over here."

He blew out a harsh breath. "I'm suffering from erectile dysfunction," he told me. I blinked; I sure as hell hadn't been expecting that. He licked his lips, rubbing his hands together, another nervous tic of his. "Apparently, I've had it since puberty since I could never hold an erection. And it's linked to my PTSD and trauma and all that other shit, so there's, like, no fucking hope for me."

I frowned at him. "Did something happen to make you feel bad about it?" He'd never mentioned it before. And I'd never heard a peep of it until now, which meant it hadn't been bothering him enough to get him down like this.

Something had happened. I knew it in my gut.

He jerked his head up at me, confused. "I just told you I have ED, and you're just... chill about it?"

I shrugged. "You have ED. Plenty of guys suffer from ED, Sterling. It's nothing to be embarrassed about, and any guy who truly loved and cared about you wouldn't care because being with you wouldn't be purely physical. There's plenty of warmth and intimacy to be had with just being together."

I'm that guy! I wanted to yell at him, but I couldn't. I couldn't risk freaking Sterling out. He needed me as much as I needed him, and I would never be selfish enough to risk ruining our friendship.

Sterling frowned. "Any guy is going to want to fuck, Graham, and that's another thing—I don't think I can," he confessed. "Darren and I tried," I gritted my teeth at the thought of him being with Darren, of Darren seeing any part of *my* man, "but I freaked out. Heard *his* voice in my head." He looked a little bit paler at the admission, and my heart cracked wide open in my chest, all the anger and jealousy abating.

"Sterling," I rasped, "look at me." It felt like it took him an eternity to do so, but he slowly raised his eyes to meet mine. "Why did you think you could manage that? You *know* you can't."

He shrugged. "He was pressuring me." *I was going to fucking bash Darren's face into the ice.* "And I just wanted to be *normal.*"

"Normal is overrated," I said, getting up from my bed. I took a seat beside him—close enough for him to feel my body heat but not so close that he felt trapped. "You're perfect just as you are, Sterling. Any guy worth your time would be perfectly fine waiting for you to be ready. And if it never happens, they would be okay with that, too."

I would be okay with it! I shouted at him in my mind. Christ, I was head over heels for him, and he'd probably never know. Because Sterling needed our friendship more than I needed to be with him. I was afraid if I confessed how I felt to him, he'd push me away. And shit, where would that leave him?

He blew out a soft breath. "Just doesn't feel like it, Graham." He leaned his head on my shoulder, and my chest loosened at the contact. Tentatively, I wrapped an arm around his shoulders, and when he didn't tense or push away, I pulled him into a hug, resting my chin on the top of his head.

"He will," I promised. I combed my fingers through his dark, curly hair, and he practically purred, his eyes shutting. It was soothing for him, and I did it as much as he allowed me to. "Promise me you won't ever do something you're not comfortable with again when it comes to other guys?"

He nodded against my shoulder. "I promise, Graham."

I dropped a kiss to the top of his head, unable to help myself. Instead of freaking out like I thought he might since I'd just pushed a major boundary, he snuggled closer.

"You make me feel safe," Sterling said softly.

I swallowed past the sudden lump in my throat, tightening my arms around him. "I'll always be your safe haven, Sterling. No matter what."

And that was a promise I'd keep until my last, dying breath.

2

Graham

I didn't want to leave Sterling by himself after our discussion. Especially not after everything he'd been through. Hearing his tormentor's voice in his head? That was scary shit. I was worried about Sterling and wanted him as close as possible so I could keep an eye on him.

But I had hockey practice, and Coach would have my ass on a silver platter if I skipped. It wouldn't matter to him that I was trying to help a friend through something. Everyone on the team knew I was bisexual, including Coach, and he'd just see it as me skipping out on practice and my team for a bit of fun.

I sighed and quickly got dressed in my gear before skating out onto the ice where most of everyone was already at. I began warming up with everyone else, trying to get my head in the game so I could make sure practice went well. I *needed* it to go well because unlike my best friend, I didn't have wealthy parents I could fall back on. Hockey was my future. Becoming part of the NHL was my sole focus—well, besides maybe trying to get my best friend to fall in love with me.

My parents had done the best for me that they could. My childhood was filled with happy memories, and they loved me dearly. I knew I could turn to them when I was in need. But financially, our lives kind of sucked. College was only part of my future because of hockey. I'd busted my ass in high school to get a full-ride scholarship. My mom, who had been working two dead-end jobs so she and Dad could afford for me to play, had burst into tears when I got my scholarship.

And to the school in the nation that had the best hockey team at that.

Dad had been working long, exhausting hours for as long as I could remember as a general laborer, and that day, when he smiled at me, I knew he thought all those exhausting days and all of the traveling he had to do for work was worth it.

And I wanted to continue to prove to my parents that supporting this dream of mine and working long, exhausting hours was not in vain.

"Bro, what the fuck is up with you?" I heard Collin ask. I glanced over to see who he was talking to and ground my teeth together at the sight of Darren next to him.

"Thought I was finally going to get some from Sterling, but the asshole can't even get hard. Can you believe that?" Darren asked him. "Fucking asshole wasn't even worth the time I spent trying to get him in bed."

I jerked to my feet, my blood pulsing hotly in my veins. "Watch what the fuck you say," I growled. I wasn't above pummeling someone on the fucking ice—not even a teammate.

He barked out a laugh. "What—you think you're going to get some from him, Graham? Good luck. He's a prude and doesn't put out for anybody. Not worth the time, if you ask—"

I body-slammed him to the ice. Grabbing the front of his helmet, I yanked his head up and smashed it back to the ice. "Don't fucking talk about him like that!" I barked.

Darren flipped me off of him before jamming his elbow into my side hard enough to knock the air from my lungs. When he tried to stand up, I kicked my legs out, knocking him back to his ass.

"Break it up!" Coach barked, storming onto the ice. "Darren, Graham, get up *now!*" he shouted.

I stood up from the ice but couldn't resist shoulder-checking Darren hard once he got up, making him stumble. The only reason he didn't fall was because Collin steadied him from the other side before quickly retreating. They all knew I wasn't one to mess with, and *everyone* on the team knew how protective I was of Sterling.

Darren was lucky I'd even let him close to my best friend, but that was before I knew how much of a fucking douchebag he was. Now, I was regretting it. Sorely. Because if I had just told Sterling that messing around with Darren wasn't a good idea, then he wouldn't be suffering right now. Sterling listened to me when it came to advice. I could've saved him from the shit he was going through.

"Both of you get in my office," Coach snarled. "The rest of you start practice."

I quickly followed behind Coach to his office, and I could feel Darren at my back, though I didn't turn to look at him. But if he opened his mouth about Sterling again, I was going to snatch that helmet off his head and bash him in his face with it.

"Sit." I dropped into a chair across from Coach's desk, and Darren took the one next to me. "I don't know what just happened out on that ice, but it will *not* happen again, am I clear? Both of you have too much going for you to allow whatever is going on to destroy your careers."

"Yes, sir," I grunted. Darren nodded.

"Boy, I cannot hear pucks rattling around inside your head," Coach snapped. "Use your voice that you were so eager to use to get Graham riled up."

"Sorry, Coach," Darren muttered, but not before he shot me a dark look. I just rolled my eyes. Asshole. "I understand."

"Good. And you'll both understand why you'll be doing extra drills after practice is over and why you'll also be helping the staff clean the rink and bleachers, yes?"

I bit back a sigh. Fuck. That was even longer I had to be away from Sterling. It made my skin crawl. But nonetheless, I nodded and said, "I understand, Coach."

Darren mumbled an affirmative as well. Coach waved us out. "Get out of my office and get back on the ice. I expect silence from both of you unless you absolutely need to speak."

We quickly left the office. Darren shot me a scathing look. "Good fucking going,

Hurley," he quietly snapped, calling me by my last name.

I cut him a side-eye. "Maybe if you weren't so busy running your mouth about Sterling, this shit wouldn't have happened."

Before he could retort even a single word, we stepped out onto the ice. I skated away from him and joined in on the drill, focusing on practice and letting everything else fade away for the moment.

That familiar tingle I usually got when my best friend was nearby raced up my spine, letting me know Sterling was watching me. I hadn't heard anyone come in, but I could just feel when he was close to me like a sixth sense. Turning around, I grinned at the sight of him—an automatic response. "Hey," I greeted, waving at him.

"You're late," he said, frowning at me. A slight grimace passed over his face before his usual mask fell into place when he saw Darren behind me, coming down the stands on the other side. "What happened?"

"Altercation," I told him with a shrug. He sighed, giving me that *look*. I hated that look; it always made me feel like a child. I chewed on my bottom lip for a moment before shooting him a sheepish smile.

"You can't go around fighting, Graham," he chastised as he came closer. "You know that. This is your *future*. Don't jeopardize that."

"Oh, look—it's *you*. Graham, man, I'm telling you. If you've been sticking around him for the past couple of years hoping to get laid," Sterling's face paled, "it's not—"

A growl rumbled through my chest, and before I even realized what I was doing, I was skating up to Sterling to close the distance between us. Gripping the back of his neck, I didn't even give myself a chance to warn him with nonverbal cues before I was bringing my face closer to his, but I stopped right before my lips met his. I would *not* contribute to the darkness in his mind. I refused to, no matter how badly I wanted to put Darren in his place.

Sterling was the one who closed the remaining distance between us, his lips softly pressing on mine. Every part of my body came alive at the feel of his smooth, warm mouth against mine. Moaning low in my throat, I gently tugged him closer, my heart racing in my chest.

Kissing Sterling was everything I had hoped it would be. And yet, it was still so much more. My lungs expanded, and it felt like every color in the world suddenly became brighter. My heart grew so much, I thought it was going to burst out of my chest.

"Fuck," Sterling whispered once we finally pulled apart to breathe. I stared at him, my soul just about ready to explode. I was so in love with him. So deep. There was no crawling out of this.

Sterling had the power to fucking destroy me. And honestly, I would let him if it meant I got to be his for even just a *minute* of my life. Hell, even just a mere *second*.

I turned to Darren, a smirk curving my lips. "Oh, he gets plenty hard," I lied to

Darren, wanting to bruise his ego. It was too damn big anyway. And he was a fucking dick for making Sterling feel like less of a man for having ED. "Turns out you just didn't do it for him."

Sterling's lips parted in surprise. Darren's face turned red, and muttering something under his breath I couldn't hear, he skated off the ice, no doubt heading to the locker room. I turned back to Sterling. "What time is it?" I asked him.

"Almost seven," he told me. I grimaced. God, it really was late, and Sterling needed to eat.

"Let me get changed," I told him, "and then we'll go grab food, yeah?"

He swallowed thickly, nodding his head at me. "And talk about that kiss?" he asked quietly, his nerves clear in his voice. God, I loved how brave he was. How he faced everything in life head-on, even if it made him nervous or scared.

I nodded. "Definitely talking about that kiss." There was no way in hell I was letting this chance slide. And it was that—a chance. It could go one of two ways, but since Sterling was the one to complete the kiss, my hopes were high that he felt the same way I did.

My fingers were crossed that I wasn't let down.

Sterling took a seat in the booth across from me, setting his plate on the table. I'd driven us to a small, buffet-style restaurant. I was hungry enough to put away an entire cow after the grueling practice I'd just suffered, and buffets were more Sterling's style when he was getting back into eating again. It gave him more options of what he could put together that wouldn't leave him feeling nauseous later.

He'd put rice with gravy, a small baked chicken leg, and green beans on his plate, which was practically nothing compared to the pile of food I had on mine. But hell, at least he was eating. That was all I could ask for when he was having rough days. It was better than not eating at all. I'd just have to make sure he snacked throughout the day tomorrow.

"So, the kiss?" he muttered, forking a green bean into his mouth right after. As if he thought if he kept his mouth occupied, he might not say anything else. It was kind of amusing actually, though I'd never tell him that.

"You know I'm bi," I reminded him.

He grunted. "Pretty sure the entire campus knows you're bi," he told me, amusement glimmering in his eyes. That was true. I'd dated other people and fucked around a good bit. Sterling had dated too, so I hadn't felt so bad about it. I never thought I would have this opportunity with Sterling.

I snickered. "I started crushing on you the moment you walked into our dorm room and said you were my roommate and told me you don't like being touched," I told him honestly. His eyes widened, and he choked on his green bean for a moment before grabbing his water and chugging some down. I waited until he set his glass down before I started speaking again. "I thought it would fade with time like my crushes normally do, but every moment I spent with you just made me like you more." I swallowed thickly. "I like you more than I've ever liked anyone, Sterling. And I know that may be a lot to swallow and digest. If you don't feel the same way, I'm okay with that. I never want to destroy our friendship."

"You like me?" he asked in astonishment. Like that was the wildest idea he'd ever heard of. As if me liking him was something impossible.

I shrugged a little. "Like might be too light of a term, but yeah. We'll go with that for now."

He set his fork down and rubbed his hands together. That nervous tic of his was so cute. "I, um, I like you, too, Graham." My heart was going to burst right out of my chest and fly up to the sky. "You're the only person outside of my parents and my therapist that can touch me, and that... that's pretty fucking incredible. I feel *safe* with you."

I held my hand out to him. His

emotions were heightened, which meant any touching needed to be on his terms. He placed his hand in mine. Curling my fingers around his hand, I gave it a gentle squeeze. "One thing I can promise you—swear on my life, in fact—is that I will *never* make you feel unsafe with me, Sterling. I will *always* be a safe haven for you."

Sterling smiled at me. "Thank you," he said quietly. "I needed to hear that more than you think."

I know, baby, I said silently. I knew Sterling better than he thought I did, but that was okay. I'd spend the rest of my life being his safe haven and taking care of him every way I could so long as he let me.

3

Sterling

"Are we watching a movie tonight?" Graham asked as he maneuvered his car into a parking spot in front of our dorm building. He'd apparently worked the entire summer before freshman year of college to save up enough money to buy a cheap car outright. And when my parents found out around Christmas of our freshman year that his insurance was about to lapse because he couldn't afford to pay it for another six months, they took over, adding him as a driver to their insurance policy, as well as his car.

Graham was still extremely grateful for their help to this day. He just asked that word never got to his parents because he didn't want them to feel bad about not being able to provide something for him. My parents and I readily agreed.

I wanted to do anything I could to help make Graham's life a little easier. He was working so hard to achieve his dreams. He'd already had a couple of offers from some NHL teams. His parents wanted him to take one of the offers, but my parents urged him to finish his college degree first, warning him an injury could take him out and that he needed something to fall back on. They'd assured him that if he kept at it, kept getting better, and kept improving, he would get offers from better teams with a higher dollar amount on his contract.

"A movie sounds good, but we both need showers first. Especially you."

He rolled his eyes at me as he shifted his car into park. "*Someone* needed to eat," he said, giving me a pointed look.

I shrugged. "We could've ordered in."

He snorted. "You needed a wider range of options," he reminded me. "We both know you struggle to eat for a couple of days after you go through something like this."

How did he know me so well? Sometimes, I thought he knew me better than I knew myself, and that was saying something. Every once in a while, he could even tell I was triggered before I was, and he worked fast to get me out of the situation without freaking me out.

I really did feel the safest with him out of everyone, even my parents, who had done everything they could to give me the safety net I needed. Who put me through therapy and gave me a comfortable life where I could work on healing and growing without being afraid every time I turned around.

"Yeah," I muttered, pushing open the car door. Graham met me at the front of his car once I got out, and when he held his hand out to me, somehow still knowing I needed to initiate touch first, I placed my hand in his, linking our fingers together before giving his hand a squeeze. It was a silent thank you. A silent appreciation for his understanding and constant patience.

"Come on. Let's go get showers so we can cuddle and watch movies."

"Cuddles," I mused, a smile tilting my lips before I could stop it. "I think I like the sound of that." Graham chuckled. I raised our hands a little as we walked inside the lobby of our dorm building, heading to the elevators. "So, what does this make us, Graham? I don't think I ever even held hands with Darren."

Graham's face screwed up in distaste. "Please keep that dick's name out of your mouth around me," he begged. "I still want to break his fucking nose." I snickered. Graham was so overprotective. I should've known he wouldn't have been able to keep his hands to himself at practice today, especially since I knew Darren was such a shit-talker. His mouth got him in a lot of trouble during games. But Graham could be just as hot-headed, especially when it came to me.

"Fine," I agreed. "Now answer my question."

"Boyfriends?" he asked, glancing over at me as we stepped into the elevator. I pressed the button for our floor and leaned back against the wall, closing my eyes and drawing in a deep breath. I hated elevators. I hated being in areas with no escape. My skin always crawled, and without a doubt, I knew I was breaking out in hives. "I'd like to be your boyfriend, Sterling. If that's what you want, that is."

I cracked open one eye, and nausea swirled in my gut. Quickly, I shut it again, drawing in a deep, shaky breath. "Yeah," I rasped. "I'd like that, too."

Graham pulled me into his arms, his hand cradling the back of my head. "Breathe, Sterling. We're almost there," he assured me. "Probably shouldn't have taken the elevator."

I grunted. "Too full to walk up five flights of stairs," I told him, burrowing my face in the crook of his neck. The scent of his cologne mixed with his sweat calmed me and cleared my head of the panic, and I breathed a little easer. "Thanks," I murmured.

"No reason to thank me," he said softly. "I'm always you're safety."

The elevator dinged, and we separated, though Graham grabbed my hand again. Quickly, we exited, and I breathed a sigh of relief before inhaling the cooler air of the hallway. Once our door was unlocked, I walked in ahead of him and flopped back on my bed for a moment.

"Christ, I hate elevators," I groaned.

Graham loomed over me, his hands in his pockets. "Just make sure you don't ride in one without me, yeah?" I nodded in agreement. It was one of our 'rules', per se. Besides, I wasn't interested in getting in an elevator without Graham there to make me feel safe. If I'd been by myself, I would've waited in the lobby on one of the chairs until my food settled more so I could climb the stairs. "I'm hopping in the shower."

He toed out of his sneakers and managed to even pull off his socks with his feet before sliding on his shower shoes. I watched as he went to his closet and pulled out a pair of sweats and boxers. He snatched a towel out of one of his drawers and then grabbed the handle of his toiletry carrier. "You good?" he asked, his hand on the door handle of our room.

I smiled at him—a real one—and his lips twitched in return, though concern was still etched into his eyes. "I'm okay," I promised.

He nodded once and slipped out of our room, quietly shutting the door behind him. Heaving a tired breath—anxiety attacks always made me exhausted, no matter how big or small they happened to be—I got off my bed and took off my sneakers and socks before putting on my shower shoes. After grabbing clothes, a towel, and my toiletry basket, I headed into the bathroom as well.

The quicker I got a shower, the quicker I could get cuddles from my boyfriend.

Boyfriend.

A stupid, goofy smile pulled at my lips as I shut the curtain separating my stall from the rest of the bathroom.

I couldn't believe Graham was *finally* my boyfriend.

Graham combed his fingers through my hair. My head was resting against his abs, and he was slouched against the wall, a bunch of pillows piled up behind him. My eyelids were drooping, but I was trying to keep them open to savor this as long as possible. Hell, I was practically on the verge of purring.

"Stop fighting it," Graham whispered. "You haven't been sleeping well. You need to get some rest."

I sighed. "Don't want to sleep yet," I mumbled, but my eyes fell shut. God, it was so hard to stay awake after an anxiety attack. And Graham was so warm and comfortable and smelled so good...

"You're safe, and I'm here," Graham promised. "Just get some sleep, Sterling."

The last thing I was aware of was him chuckling at something in the movie and his fingers still combing through my hair, his nails lightly scratching my scalp.

The light was blinding. My eyeballs were screaming in pain, but for some reason, I couldn't shut them. My retinas were burning, desperately in need of moisture and darkness.

"Pretty boy," he whispered, his voice bouncing off the walls and seeming to echo in my mind. "Such a pretty boy, aren't you, Sterling? Are you going to be good for Daddy? He's missed you."

"No," I mumbled. Fear sliced through my veins. I tried to will my legs to move or my head to turn so I could find him, but I couldn't do anything. "I'm an adult. You don't want me anymore."

"Oh, but I do, pretty boy. We have so many years to make up for, Sterling. I've missed you so much."

Vomit rose in my throat, and I gagged, trying to swallow it back down. My heart was racing. Sweat beaded along my skin, making my clothes stick to me. I wanted to run, but my body wouldn't move. Why wouldn't my body move?

"Sterling..." he murmured, suddenly right in my ear.

"Go away," I pleaded. I couldn't breathe. Why couldn't I breathe? What the fuck was sitting on my chest?

"Sterling..." he said in my ear again, this time louder. I whimpered, a sob rising in my throat. This couldn't be happening again.

"Sterling!" he suddenly shouted.

I jerked awake, my eyes snapping open. The room was dark, just how I preferred it. Graham wasn't touching me, but he was close. I could *feel* his proximity to me. His heat emanated onto me, burning me in the best way possible.

A shiver raced down my spine as I sucked in desperate lungfuls of air. Finally, I turned my head, looking at Graham. He was laying beside me, his eyes intent on my features. I closed my eyes again, shivers suddenly wracking my body. My teeth began to chatter. I was hot, but I felt so cold on the inside.

It'd felt so fucking *real*.

"Breathe," Graham whispered. "Just focus on breathing, Sterling. You're safe. Everything is okay. He can't touch you anymore."

Logically, I knew that. He was still in prison for what he'd done to me and numerous other kids who'd eventually succumbed to their injuries and been buried in his backyard. He'd even had a whole small graveyard for them all, which had helped put him behind bars for even longer.

But trying to tell that to the fear pulsing through me, *choking me*, was near impossible.

I scooted closer to Graham, and when I pressed my body fully to his, he immediately wrapped me up in his arms, holding me tightly. His fingers began that soothing, rhythmic combing through my hair. We lay like that for what had to be at least an hour. It took a while for my teeth to stop chattering and even longer for my body to stop shaking. Eventually, the fear dissipated, and I relaxed in Graham's arms.

"That's it," he murmured. "He can *never*

touch you again, Sterling. *Never.* Because I'll never let him come near you again."

I nodded. "I know," I rasped. I pressed a kiss to his throat, and he shivered, drawing in a deep, shaky breath at the small, intimate touch. "Thank you for being here."

He tightened his hold on me, his actions saying everything he didn't in words.

Always.

4

Graham

Waking up with Sterling in my arms immediately brightened my day. If I got to wake up like this every morning, I could definitely become a morning person. The alarm would have to go though. Alarms automatically dimmed my mood a bit. There was just something about waking up to an annoying blaring sound that automatically made me grumpy.

"Turn it off," Sterling muttered, rolling away from me and shoving his head beneath a pillow.

I quickly grabbed my phone and cut off the alarm before dropping it back onto the nightstand and rubbing my gritty eyes. Fuck, I was tired, but it was Saturday morning, which meant I had hockey practice. Every Saturday, I wondered if hockey was worth getting up at this stupid hour—six A.M.—but normally by the time I was done with warm-ups, I remembered why I was okay with six A.M. hockey practice on a Saturday.

I loved being on the ice, and this was my future. If I wanted it, I had to fight for it.

Sterling's snore met my ears, and I quietly chuckled before I rolled out of bed, planting my feet on the comfy rug between our beds. When we'd been partnered up freshman year as dorm-mates, I'd come with the bare necessities—clothes, laptop, school books, and bed sheets. Then, Sterling had shown up with all kinds of shit—this fuzzy rug, lamps, *two* laptops (one to remain in the dorm and one to carry to classes), a mini-fridge, a microwave, and a toaster.

His mom had spoiled the hell out of us,

and I was proud to say she considered me to be her other son. I didn't take that kind of welcome lightly, especially when I knew just how cautious Sterling's parents were about letting people in. For them, Sterling always came first, and if someone didn't check off certain points in their books, then they were just kind of kept at arm's length.

I'd, thankfully, passed all of their little tests without even knowing they had any.

Moving quietly, I grabbed a pair of socks and slipped them on my feet before tugging a shirt over my head. After grabbing a hoodie and tugging it on over my t-shirt, I grabbed my bag, shoved my feet into my shoes, and quietly slipped out of the dorm room, already thinking about where Sterling and I could go for breakfast after practice.

Sue me—I was hungry. And Sterling's mom and dad always made sure Sterling had more than enough money for us to eat at places other than what was served on campus because they knew how Sterling's eating habits were.

Again—they spoiled the hell out of us.

It'd been hard to get used to at first, but I'd finally come around. And I knew my parents were more than thankful that I was getting to experience other things, even if they couldn't be the ones to provide it for me.

Coach's whistle blew, signaling a break so we could hydrate. Despite the cooler temperature of the arena, I was sweating, as were most of my other teammates. Collin was one of the lucky few who hardly *ever* sweated unless a game was particularly grueling.

"You good, man?" Collin asked, clapping his hand to my back as I poured water into my mouth.

I looked over at him, lowering my water bottle as I did so. A frown tugged at my lips. "Yeah, I'm good," I assured him. "Why?"

"You've been kind of quiet. Not normally like you."

I had a lot on my mind—particularly the man still sleeping in my bed. I couldn't stop thinking about him—how he was now my boyfriend, which was surreal in itself, that he'd *kissed* me even if I'd sort of initiated it to begin with, how he'd allowed me to touch him and hold him while he had so much turmoil inside of him last night.

That last one was a *huge* step of progress. Even now, my throat tightened at how much that meant to me. It meant he trusted me more than he trusted anyone else in the world—even his own parents because he still wouldn't let them touch him when he woke up from nightmares and flashbacks.

I knew how fragile that trust was, and I also knew how easily it could be broken.

"Just thinking about some stuff," I told him. "Nothing to worry about, man. My head is still one hundred percent in the game."

"Probably more up Sterling's ass," Darren muttered. I didn't think he meant for me to hear it, but I did regardless. I swung my glare to him, and Collin quickly put a hand against my chest.

"Watch your fucking mouth," I warned him.

"Not today," Collin said just as another teammate stepped in front of Darren, saying something to him I couldn't quite make out. "Let it go. He's bitter as fuck. That's it. Let him stew in his own shit."

I rolled my shoulders and stiffly nodded my head. But if Darren thought he could continue to be funny, I'd show him I was fucking hilarious.

I could take any other shit. I could let just about anything else roll off my shoulders if I really wanted. But not when it came to Sterling.

I'd start a fucking war over my man.

"Bro," Dash, one of my teammates, said quietly as he quickly made his way over to where I was pulling my shirt over my head. I was more than ready to get back to the dorm and go get breakfast with Sterling. I'd already showered after practice because there was no way in hell I was taking the short ride back to our dorm building with my sweat clinging to my skin. That was just fucking gross. Besides, it meant that once I saw Sterling, I didn't have to let him out of my sight again to shower.

"Yeah?" I asked, turning to face him.

My impatience must have shown on my face because he winced. "Look, I know you like to get out of here as quickly as possible to go get breakfast with Sterling, but you need to see this."

Oh, this couldn't be good. My gut told me so, and it was hardly ever wrong. And I also had a feeling it had to do with Sterling. Because if it was about me, they'd have been ribbing me over it.

Dash held his phone out to me, and I took it, glancing down at the social media post. My teeth audibly ground together when I saw the picture of Sterling. He was shirtless, sweat clinging to his skin as he ran on a treadmill. I could see rain sliding down the window behind him, so it hadn't been taken today. And right next to that picture, someone had posted another picture that was zeroed in on his crotch.

The caption read, *When you can't get your dick up.*

Snarling, I pushed past Dash, shoving his phone against his chest as I did so. Darren was closing his locker when I walked up to him. Gripping the back of his neck, I shoved him against it, my muscles bulging with the urge to bash his skull into the metal.

"Did you fucking do that shit?" I barked, tightening my hold when he tried to push back. "You post that bullshit on social media about Sterling?"

"What? No!" he shouted. "I don't even know what you're talking about, Graham! Fucking let go of me, dammit!"

"Don't fucking lie to me!" I yelled at him. Our teammates were trying to tug me back, but it was a fruitless cause. "I know it was you! You just had to go running your mouth and starting fucking rumors!"

Collin and Dash finally yanked me off of him. My chest was heaving. I tightened my hands into fists at my sides, baring my teeth at Darren when he turned to face me. With a shaking hand, I pointed my finger at his face. "You shut that shit down *now*, Darren, or so help me God, I'll break both of your fucking legs and ruin your entire hockey career." I yanked myself out of Dash's and Collin's grips. "Fucking let go of me," I snarled.

I stormed back over to my locker and slammed it closed before storming out of the locker room, not even bothering to grab my gym bag. I'd come back for it later.

Right then, the only thing on my mind was getting to Sterling as fast as possible to try to brace him for the shit storm Darren had caused with his big mouth.

Fuck!

Sterling was MIA when I stepped into our dorm room. His phone was on his bed, but his running shoes were missing. Cursing and silently threatening to beat the fuck out of Darren for causing this mess, I turned and sprinted down the hall to the stairs. Once I was back in my car, I quickly backed out—almost right into another car in my rush—and tore off down the street to hunt him down.

He couldn't be far if he left on foot. That was what I was hoping anyway, but I had no way of knowing unless I went to the parking garage, which was where I headed first. The only time he used his car was when he had a therapy appointment or he went home to visit his family for a couple of days when he had breaks or on the weekends, which was rare in itself.

When I entered the parking garage, I sagged a little in relief when I saw his car still sitting in its usual spot. It hadn't been moved since he parked it there last. It gave me more hope that I'd be able to find him easier—just needed to check his usual haunts first.

Sterling was a man of routine, and I had a feeling that wouldn't change, even if he'd no doubt seen the social media post about him. I was pretty sure that was why he'd gone running. He wasn't ready to face everyone knowing something so personal about him. And putting him down for it.

One would think being in college

meant we didn't have to deal with childish bullshit like this, but nope. If anything, it was even worse.

My hands white-knuckled the steering wheel as I slowly drove around campus where Sterling frequented. Finally, I found him running laps around the track field. He didn't come here often, which was why it was one of the last places I'd checked. And it was nearly empty, which explained why he'd come here.

Quickly, I parked my car and swung out of the driver's seat before jogging into the entrance, running to catch up with him. He looked over at me in surprise when I fell into step next to him, and then a sort of peace fell over his features, a small smile tilting his lips, the shadows momentarily disappearing from his dark eyes.

I returned the smile, ignoring the worry constricting my chest for the time being. For now, he just needed to know he wasn't alone, that I wasn't going anywhere.

So, for the next hour, we continued to jog around the track until he felt like he'd outrun whatever was chasing him. Near the entrance to the track, he stopped, his chest rapidly rising and falling, sweat running down his face. And surprising the hell out of me, he turned and wrapped his arms around my shoulders, burrowing his face in the crook of my neck.

My chest loosened as I quickly enveloped him in my arms, pressing a tender kiss to his temple.

"I'm always here, baby," I said softly, the term of endearment slipping out before I could stop it. But the way he shivered in my arms and stepped closer, pressing us together, I knew it was the right thing to say.

5

Sterling

The water pulsed down over my back, washing the sweat and grime off my skin from my run. Exhaustion was sitting like a heavy weight on my shoulders. Today had been a shit-tastic day, despite it starting off great. I'd woken up in Graham's bed, wrapped up in his blankets and swarmed with his pillows. The scent of him had been clinging to my skin and clothes, relaxing me. I'd even made so much progress by letting him comfort me and hold me after my nightmare last night.

Then, I'd logged onto social media, like I did every Saturday morning while waiting on Graham to finish hockey practice, and the first post I'd seen was two pics of me. One was okay—I actually looked kind of hot. The second pic, someone had zoomed in on my dick and made a disgusting comment.

When you can't get your dick up.

It was still running through my head on a fucking loop. I couldn't get it out.

The number of reactions and comments on that post had sent me spiraling, and a panic attack had grabbed hold of me, dragging me into its dangerous riptide. There'd been no hope for me, and it'd been a struggle to bring myself out of it.

When I did—with tears running down my face and my teeth chattering—I'd shoved my feet into my shoes and did the only thing I knew to do.

Run. Run from my demons. Run from that fucking post.

Just *run*. As far and as fast as I could.

Graham showing up had been a lifesaver. He'd kept pace with me the entire time, not once complaining even though I knew he'd just finished practice. Then, silently, he'd held me when I hugged him, desperate to feel his arms around me. Because with Graham, I knew everything was okay. I was safe, and no one could touch me.

The car ride back to our dorm building had been silent, but he had held my hand the entire way. We even took the stairs up to the fifth floor instead of using the elevators. Then, he'd simply pressed a kiss to my lips and left me to gather my clothes for a shower.

I leaned my head back, letting the water drench my hair. I just wanted to go to sleep. Or at least curl up in bed with Graham where the rest of the cruel, harsh world couldn't touch me for a little while. Because Graham wouldn't let it.

I quickly washed my hair and body before turning the water off and stepping into the area to dry off and get dressed. "Babe, you okay in there?" Graham asked from the other side of the curtain.

"Yeah," I rasped. I cleared my throat

before attempting to speak again. "I'll meet you in the dorm room."

I heard him walk off a moment later. After tugging on my sweats, I towel-dried my hair. Once it was no longer dripping, I tossed my towel over my bare shoulder and grabbed my basket of toiletries before heading to our dorm room up the hall. When I walked in, Graham was reclined back in bed, his hair damp, his torso bare. Nothing but a pair of boxers was riding low on his hips, revealing the V of his hips.

Good fucking Lord, he was hot as hell.

"Come on," he coaxed, patting the spot beside him. "I've already got a movie ready to go."

I smiled at him as I hung my towel up to dry so it wouldn't be mildewed when I put it in the laundry and set my toiletries on the counter. I crawled over him and settled by the wall before resting my head on Graham's chest. He wound an arm around me and pressed play on the movie.

I walked my fingers over his abs, not even paying attention to whatever he had on. I just needed to touch him. Pleasurable tingles ran through my body, but my dick wasn't getting hard despite it. Still, I wanted to touch Graham however I could, even if I got nothing in return.

"Sterling," he rumbled when I teased the waistband of his boxers. His fingers dug into my flesh, but instead of feeling trapped, I pressed closer, wanting more. I loved how he touched me. Loved how special I felt when he looked at me. When he held me like this.

"I want to," I pleaded, looking up at him.

He leaned down and kissed me. It started slow and soft, but it didn't take long for it to grow more heated. He slid his tongue into my mouth, and I moaned. Sliding my hand beneath the waistband of his boxers, I circled my hand around his cock. He was hard and smooth, his tip wet with precum.

"*Oh, fuck*," Graham groaned. He rolled to the side, drawing me closer, trapping my hand between us. But that was fine because he began to thrust into my hand, moaning into my mouth. His tongue was hot and wet, and his cock was hard as steel, even more precum leaking from the mushroom-tipped head.

"Your cock feels so good," I rasped into his mouth.

"Tighter," he panted. I tightened my fist around him, and he snarled my name, thrusting even faster. By this point, we were barely even kissing anymore. He was just panting into my mouth, our tongues half-heartedly licking as he chased his orgasm.

"Sterling!" he shouted right before his cum spilled into my fist and wet the front of his boxers. I slid the fingers of my free hand into his hair and softly kissed him, gently working him down from his high. He finally pushed my hand away, and I brought my fingers to my lips, licking his cum off. He groaned, his eyes shutting for a brief moment before he opened them to continue watching me.

I moaned at the taste of him. Christ, I should've given him head instead. I would be mourning that loss for the rest of the night.

"That's hot," Graham whispered.

I smiled and sat up before sliding off the bed to go wash my hands. "Next time, I'm giving you head."

Graham groaned as he slid out of bed, dropping his boxers. I bit my lip at the sight of his toned ass in the mirror. "That's teasing because now I've got the image of you sucking my dick in my head."

I snickered. But the intimacy we'd shared had settled the turmoil inside of me. I was calm. Warm. Safe.

When I slid back into bed, Graham immediately curled his body around mine, his warm breath fanning the skin on the back of my neck. I covered his hand with one of mine, my eyes sliding closed.

This—this right here—was all I needed in life.

🥢

"Why is your phone ringing this early?" Graham groaned, burrowing his face in my shoulder.

"Just ignore it," I mumbled, tugging the blanket over my face. It was too fucking early to be awake after the day I'd ended up having yesterday. I wanted to lay in bed all day and just sleep and pretend the world didn't exist and that people weren't talking shit about my ED on social media.

My phone finally stopped ringing, but then it started right back up again. Graham cursed and rolled away from me. A pathetic whine slid from between my lips. I wasn't ready to be separated from him yet. Every time I'd started having a nightmare, Graham had somehow coaxed me out of it without waking me up too much, so I easily fell back asleep every time. I wanted his warmth back around me so I could sleep some more.

"It's your mom," Graham grumbled, putting the phone in front of me on the mattress. As he wrapped his body back around me, crushing me to him, I cracked one eye open and answered the call, putting it on speaker after so I didn't have to hold the damn thing.

My eyes sliding closed, I croaked, "Hey."

"Hey, hun!" Mom exclaimed, much too

chipper for how early it was. I groaned, making her release a breezy little laugh. "We're in town. Wanted to have breakfast with you and Graham, if the two of you are up to it."

Graham's stomach rumbled behind me at the mention of breakfast. It didn't matter that he was barely awake right now. His stomach was, and it had a mind of its own. And Graham usually ended up following it.

"Does it include pancakes that my Coach will kill me for?" Graham sleepily asked. "Because if so, I'm one hundred percent in."

Mom snorted. "Yes, Graham, it includes pancakes."

I groaned again. It was clear I was now on the losing side. "I guess we're meeting you for breakfast," I muttered.

"Oh, don't sound so down about it," Mom teased. "You love it when I surprise you and wake you up."

I really didn't, though I did enjoy her and Dad's company. They weren't overbearing parents—just protective. And after the hell I'd gone through, that protection was welcome. I knew it definitely wasn't easy for Mom to let me come to college away from home, but she was comforted by the fact that my therapist was nearby. And when I became friends with Graham, she relaxed even more.

I had a system here—a reliable one. And that was all she wanted for me.

"Meet us at that breakfast spot down the road from campus," Mom instructed. "I can't think of the name of it right now. Graham knows which one I'm talking about."

"If anything pertains to food, he always knows," I joked, slowly coming more awake.

Graham lightly bit my shoulder, making me yelp. "Stop teasing Graham, Sterling," Mom scolded, but her tone was too light to actually be serious. "We'll see you in, say... an hour?"

"An hour's good," I assured her. When the call ended, I rolled over and narrowed my eyes at Graham. "Did you seriously fucking *bite* me?"

Graham just grinned. Then, he rolled

us over so I was beneath him, settling between my thighs. My body came alive, though not one hundred percent like I would've preferred. But when his lips met mine, I ceased to care.

All I could think about was the way Graham's body weight felt pressing me into the mattress and how warm and wet his mouth was. Moaning, I mapped the planes of his muscled back with my fingertips and palms, my legs binding around his hips to keep him secured to me. He was hard—I could feel his shaft pressing against my belly—but he was ignoring it, instead just slowly kissing me. Taking his time like I was something precious to be treasured. Like I was the rarest gem in the world and he had to protect me and take care of me at all costs.

"You're so fucking mine," Graham groaned into my mouth before making his way across my jaw.

A breathless chuckle spilled from my lips. "So fucking yours?" I rasped, admiring the way his muscles flexed in his back as he moved.

"Fuck yes," he groaned. "*Mine*. I've waited so damn long for you. A little over two years has felt like a fucking eternity, Sterling." He moved back to my lips, kissing me again. I groaned, my fingertips pressing into his skin.

"You're mine, too," I panted when we parted. My eyes met his. His hazel eyes were blazing with need and adoration, and butterflies erupted in my stomach at the tender yet lustful look.

Graham traced my jaw with the tips of his fingers. "I'll always be yours, Sterling," he vowed. "*Always*."

"I'm fucking starving," Graham grumbled beneath his breath as we stepped into the restaurant hand-in-hand, our fingers linked together. "It smells so fucking good in here." Graham's stomach rumbled in agreement with its host.

At this point, his stomach felt almost like a parasite. Graham was *always* hungry.

And I had no idea where he managed to put it all.

"Oh, my *God*!" Mom squealed as we neared the table she and Dad were sitting at. Her eyes were wide and hopeful, and she was practically bouncing in her seat beside Dad. Dad was quietly chuckling at her antics. "Are you two *finally* together? We've been shipping you two since you met," Mom gushed.

My face flamed red. Graham snickered and pressed a kiss to my cheek before pulling my chair out for me. I quietly thanked him and sat down. Once he took his seat beside me, he draped his arm over the back of my chair and ran his fingertips up and down my shoulder. "Yeah, we're together." Graham turned his head and winked at me. "Finally."

Mom squealed again and then quickly pulled out her phone, her manicured fingers quickly flying over her screen. Dad shook his head in amusement. "I'm glad the two of you are happy," Dad told us. "You're good for our boy, Graham. We wouldn't dare trust him with another soul."

Graham cleared his throat, his expression solemn. "I know, Mr. Hardison. I don't take that lightly."

I placed my hand on his thigh and gave it a gentle squeeze. He glanced over at me, and the tips of his lips curved up the tiniest bit into a smile. My chest squeezed.

I was so in love with him. Head over heels. Drowning in it. And I never wanted to inhale anything but his ocean ever again.

"Honey, can you stop texting Graham's mother for two seconds so you can decide what to order?" Dad asked her. I snickered. Graham's mom and my mom were thick as thieves since they met the summer between our freshman and sophomore years. Graham wanted to hang out with me, but my mom was wary of letting me spend so much time at someone's house with parents she'd never met before, so Graham spent a month at my house while my mom and Graham's mom got to know each other, and then I spent a month at his.

Fuck, we'd been nearly inseparable since meeting freshman year.

"How are classes going?" Dad asked us.

As he spoke, he slowly slid Mom's phone over to him when she set it down and pocketed it. I coughed to cover my laugh, but Graham wasn't as discreet.

"Did you just take my phone?" Mom snapped at him. "Trish and I were having a conversation about our boys and planning their marriage."

I knew she was teasing, but I still gaped at her. "Mom!" I snapped. Graham's shoulders were shaking from his laughter. I glowered at him. "Stop it," I hissed at him. "It's not funny."

"It kind of is," he told me, a grin on his lips. He ran the tips of his fingers over the side of my neck, and I shivered. "Make no mistake about it, Sterling, I'm marrying you one day."

I gaped at him next. Mom shrieked, so excited she almost spilled her glass of orange juice. Dad sighed and moved it back, so used to her being hyper all the time that it was second nature for him.

"Can we confess our love first?" I croaked.

Graham winked at me. "Oh, we will.

But not in the middle of a diner with your parents as an audience."

I was lost for words. One hundred percent. The only thing I managed was a choking sound. My heart was about to beat out of my chest, and my stomach was full of the whole fucking zoo. Breakfast? Who the hell needed breakfast when Graham was sitting here teasing me with promises of a big future where he was by my side the entire way?

"Oh, look—having breakfast with your doctor to help your *problem*?" Darren suddenly hissed from beside me.

My face paled. I didn't want my parents to know about my ED. One, it was super embarrassing. But two, they would be wounded that I hadn't been able to confide in them about this for *years*. And they'd be upset that I'd hidden it from them since puberty, especially since it pertained to my health.

"First of all," Dad said calmly, looking up at Darren before Graham or I could say a word, "we're not his doctors. We're his parents." Darren paled a little. "Second of all, I don't know what problem you have with my son, but I suggest you drop it. He's not one you want to mess with, kid. Because I'll ruin your entire hockey career, do you understand me?"

My dad knew he was on the hockey team?

Darren looked ready to pass out. My dad had more money than he'd ever spend in one lifetime due to generational wealth. And my mother had built her business from the ground up selling t-shirts of all things, and now she was a self-made millionaire in her own right. Darren had no idea who they were messing with.

"It won't happen again," Darren mumbled before he quickly moved away, grabbing the arm of the guy he was with to tug him away.

"Well, that went well. I won't have to break his legs now," Graham mused, reaching for his water.

I cut my boyfriend a dark look. "You won't touch him," I warned him. "Your hockey career is too important."

"He's right," Mom agreed with me. I

smirked at Graham. He just rolled his eyes at me. "If anyone is giving you or Sterling a problem, bring it to us. It'll be handled. You have a lot riding on hockey, and you don't need to do anything to potentially ruin that. Clear?"

"Clear," Graham quietly agreed.

"How did you know he played hockey?" I asked Dad.

Dad smirked and shot a pointed look at Graham, whose ears colored a light red in embarrassment. And probably a little shame. "Graham vented to Trish about you and Darren seeing each other, and of course, Trish told your mother, who told me. I did a background check on him."

I sighed and leaned my head back to stare up at the ceiling. Graham propped his chin on my shoulder, and I turned to look at him. Ours lips were so close, I only had to move a hair for them to brush together. My boyfriend was giving me sweet puppy-dog eyes, and my frustration melted away.

"You aren't mad at me, are you?"

I sighed and pressed a small kiss to his lips, making him smile. My heart melted in my chest. "No, Graham, I'm not mad at you. Our parents are just very big gossipers."

Mom gasped, placing her hand on her chest in mock hurt. "I object. That's offensive."

Dad snorted, and I barked out a laugh.

6

Sterling

The lights above me were too bright. My retinas throbbed in pain, but I couldn't close my eyes—not when he had my eyelids taped open. Hot tears spilled down the sides of my face as his hand crept along my leg.

"Please don't," I pleaded when he rolled me onto my stomach. "Daddy, it hurts when you do that," I cried. It always felt like he was ripping me apart, and I always bled.

"You're Daddy's pretty boy," he rasped from behind me. "And I want to touch my pretty boy." I shook my head, choking on a sob.

A knock sounded on the old, wooden front door, making it rattle, and he moved back from me, his touch disappearing. I sobbed in relief, snot running down my face and pooling onto the race car bed sheets beneath me that he had just washed this morning. I was already ruining them.

"Oh, hey," I heard him greet whoever was at the door. "I forgot you were coming today. You got the money? No payment, no play."

"Of course, I've got the fucking money," a raspy voice replied. "Here. Now where's the boy?"

I scrambled off the bed, rushing to the closet to escape whatever was about to happen. I knew it wouldn't be good. Any time he had friends over, it hurt so much. And I bled even more than usual.

"Oh, no you don't, boy," the stranger suddenly growled. I hadn't even heard him enter my bedroom. He snatched me back by my hair, and I screamed, my chest wracking with sobs as he dragged me back over to my bed. "I paid for you, and I want my fucking money's worth."

I shot upright, sweat drenching me.

Tears were streaming down my cheeks, and I hiccupped, snot running down my nose. Not even caring that I might wake Graham, I kicked the comforter off of me and crawled out of bed, landing on my hands and knees on the floor. I gagged, and vomit spewed from between my lips.

"Baby, baby—fuck, you're okay. You're safe," Graham cooed, settling beside me on the floor without touching me. Our rug was ruined, and that made me sad as fuck, but there was no way I had been capable of making it to the bathroom or even just to the sink or the fucking trashcan by the door. My knees were weak, and my legs were shaking.

I leaned back and settled on my ass, dragging my knees to my chest. "The rug —" I croaked.

"I'll call your mom and get it cleaned. I'll even tell her I was the one who threw up so she doesn't hound you about what happened, okay?" He held out one of his t-shirts that he'd grabbed off the floor. "Here. Clean your face up, baby. And just breathe."

I grabbed it from him, too rattled to care about ruining one of his shirts, and wiped the vomit from around my lips before folding it to wipe the snot and tears from my cheeks. My entire body hurt from that fucking nightmare—flashback, really—and my ass clenched in phantom pain. Once my face was cleaned, Graham grabbed the shirt from me and tossed it across the room into the trash can. Had I been my normal self, I'd have said something along the lines of "Score!", but instead, I leaned back against the side of his bed and closed my eyes, dragging deep breaths into my aching lungs.

When Graham settled beside me, close enough that his body heat was burning me but not so close that any part of him was touching me, I scooted over. Immediately, he dropped his legs, and I turned my body, climbing over him so I could straddle his thighs. Wrapping my arms around his shoulders, I burrowed my face in the crook of his neck. Immediately, his arms wrapped around my back, and he clutched me to him. I sank into his hold, letting him warm my soul in a way nothing else could.

"I had a flashback," I croaked.

Graham's hands coasted up and down my back in long, gentle strokes. "With how violently you responded, I figured," he said softly. "You should go see your therapist in the morning."

I nodded in agreement. "I will," I promised. "I need to brush my teeth. I know my breath reeks, but I don't want to move yet."

Graham squeezed me to him, and he moved one of his hands to my hair, combing his fingers through it in a slow, rhythmic motion. I clenched his hips with my thighs, clinging to him. "Then you stay right here for as long as you need, Sterling."

Tears began to slide down my cheeks again, but he just continued holding me as I drenched his skin in my pain. In my torment. He never said a word, but I didn't need him to. Being able to cry while resting in the safest place for me on the planet was cathartic.

Dr. Clancy's brows were furrowed in concern as I stepped through the door that led into the back of her office building where each individual therapy office was located. "Random appointments twice in such little time is alarming, Sterling," she said softly.

I nodded in agreement. "I know. And I'm freaking out a bit," I admitted. I hadn't been back to sleep yet, which meant Graham didn't either. He just put on a movie last night once we crawled back into bed to keep my mind distracted and held me. He ran his fingers through my hair for *hours* until Dr. Clancy's office opened and I was able to make an appointment. Which meant we'd both missed our first classes of the day.

"What's going on?" she asked once we were in her office. I took a seat on the couch and rubbed my palms together, feeling jittery. "You were doing so well until this incident with Darren."

I knew that, too. I shouldn't have

pushed myself like I had, especially when I knew I didn't feel safe with him. It had been careless and a stupid decision on my part. Now, I was dealing with the consequences.

And those consequences were terrifying the fuck out of me.

"I had a flashback," I quietly told her. "It was just nightmares every night, but last night, that changed. Most of my memories from back then are blocked, but I *know* that night happened. I felt the terror. The pain. *His* touch. I felt it all. Recalled it. And now it's stuck here," I croaked, pressing my fingers to my temples. My leg began to bounce. "It won't go away."

"First, breathe," she commanded. I sucked in a deep breath, even though it hurt to do so when my lungs were being squeezed so tightly. "Good. Keep breathing," she ordered. "And ground yourself. I know you're scared, Sterling, but you are *safe* here, and you know that. Otherwise, you wouldn't have come to me."

I knew she was right, but my mind

wasn't grasping that concept. I felt displaced. Torn apart. Vulnerable.

I pressed my fingertips against my eyelids, shuddering when I remembered them being taped open. I swallowed back vomit and forced my breathing to regulate so we could continue this appointment. I needed help. I was desperate.

"I want to try a new medication," I rasped, looking up at her finally. Dr. Clancy nodded. "I'm desperate. I need help. I can't live like this."

"Okay," she said gently. "I'll write you a prescription for Xanax before you leave here today. Get it filled immediately and take it every night before you go to bed. It'll help your anxiety, which will also help you sleep better and hopefully ward off the nightmares and flashbacks you're having. Just be aware it may take up to two weeks to go into effect, Sterling." She gave me a pointed look because I was one of those patients that expected everything to work immediately.

I nodded. "Okay," I said quietly. If it wasn't working in two weeks, I'd give up again. But *maybe* this one would work for me. Especially since I had to take it at nighttime rather than the daytime pills she'd prescribed me when I was younger, which made me feel all out of sorts. Some even made me feel like a zombie. I'd even taken one that made me drool, and I refused to go to school until it stopped.

"Do you feel like you can talk about the flashback with me?" she gently asked. "If you can't, that's okay. We can work our way up to it at your next appointment."

I shook my head. "I don't want to," I confessed. "But I will. Because I feel like that memory is choking the fuck out of me —excuse my language."

She waved me off. "Free space in my office, remember? Sometimes, the added fuck is needed."

I smiled a little. "I don't know how old I was," I told her. She linked her fingers together, all of her attention on me. "But my bed was wooden, and I had racecar bedsheets." I blinked, shuddering. For a moment, I'd been right back in that room, and my skin crawled. "And my eyelids were taped open. The room was so bright. I don't know why. But it felt like there were a billion fucking lights shining down on me." I shuddered, a chill sweeping down my spine.

Right then, I was more thankful than I'd ever been that she kept her office dark.

"He was touching me. And I panicked when he rolled me onto my stomach because it always hurt." Even now, my ass clenched with that phantom pain again like it had last night. "I was pleading with him. And then someone knocked on the door. There was talk about money, and the stranger asked where I was." I rubbed the back of my skull where a phantom ache began at the memory of that man grabbing me by my hair and dragging me back to my bed. "I tried running, but it didn't work."

"What happened?" Dr. Clancy gently pushed.

I swallowed more vomit. I was surprised I could even throw up considering I hadn't eaten anything in over twelve hours now. "He, um, grabbed me by my hair and dragged me back to the bed," I whispered.

"I woke up before I could live through any more of it, but I know what happened. I fucking *remember* it." I gagged and rushed to the trashcan by her door, throwing up into it.

When I was done throwing up nothing but stomach acid and the little bit of water Graham had managed to get in my body this morning, she handed me a stick of spearmint gum, which I quickly shoved into my mouth. I sat back down on the couch. "I'd like to stop there," I quietly requested.

Dr. Clancy nodded. "We'll stop there then," she said. "But I want to do this exercise with you before you leave today, okay?" I blew out a soft breath. Sometimes, her exercises drained everything out of me, but they helped. Even if I felt close to death afterward sometimes.

"Close your eyes, Sterling." I did as she instructed. "It's going to hurt," I grunted, "but I want you to go back to that day in your mind—to the part you can't tell me about." I tensed, my stomach churning. But I trusted her, so I did as she asked. "I want you to wrap your younger self in your arms and hold him as he's being hurt. I want you to make sure he's not alone. It won't make the pain go away, but it'll make it bearable."

Hot tears slid down my cheeks as I wrapped the younger version of me in my arms and held him as he was violated and raped. As he bled on his racecar bedsheets. As he screamed and begged for them to stop.

And fuck, I cried with him. Because no little boy—no human being on the fucking earth—should have to go through what he did. What *we* did.

When I opened my eyes, Dr. Clancy was watching me with a proud look on her face. "You okay?"

I nodded and swiped at my cheeks. "I think I've had enough for today," I rasped.

She tore off a script from her prescription pad and handed it to me. I folded it and stuck it in my pocket. "Start those tonight," she ordered. "And try to take them at the same time."

"I will." I stood. "Thank you for seeing me."

"Thank you for coming to me, Sterling. That takes real strength."

I nodded and left. After dropping off my prescription at the pharmacy on campus, I walked a few laps around the building, waiting for it to be filled, too worked up to sit still. And once I'd gone through the new medication consultation with the pharmacist on staff and had my pills in my pocket, I parked my car in the parking garage and began the walk to the hockey arena.

Graham would be at practice, and while I knew he couldn't actually be with me, I could still be close to him. And right then, I needed Graham any way I could have him.

Graham

I pushed the puck across the ice to Dash, who quickly sent it sailing into the net. Coach blew his whistle, shouting something at our defense.

"Hey, your boy is here," Collin said as he skated past me.

Immediately, I looked up into the bleachers, and sure enough, Sterling was sitting right behind the plexiglass, his hood pulled up on his jacket. His head was bent forward, no doubt asleep. My heart ached for him. I knew today wasn't a good day for him, and I wanted nothing more than to say fuck practice and take him back to our dorm so I could cuddle in bed with him.

But then he'd be angry with me for skipping out on practice. And I couldn't stand it when Sterling was upset with me. It felt like the world was ending when he was.

"Graham!" Coach barked. I wanted to bare my teeth at him for yelling when my boyfriend was finally getting some fucking rest, but I bit back my anger. "Focus," he snapped at me.

I nodded once. "Sorry, Coach." I quickly got into position to begin the next drill, forcing myself to focus on practice and block out everything else, even if it wasn't easy. But if I wanted to give Sterling the future he deserved, then I needed to put my all into this sport.

Even if it made me feel like I was neglecting him in the process.

Darren didn't say a word to me at all during practice except for plays and to get my attention, but only when it was absolutely necessary. I also knew he'd spotted Sterling, but he'd just quickly looked away, not saying a word on that either.

Maybe Mr. Hardison finally put the fear of God into that asshole.

I quickly showered and changed, probably the fastest I ever had in my life, and then rushed out of the locker room to go wake up Sterling. I'd come up with an idea during practice, and I was hoping he'd like it. It would be cold, but it would also be dark and peaceful, which I knew Sterling craved. Especially after last night. I had no doubt he'd been trapped in a bright ass room in that violent memory.

Too much light really bothered him now because of it. It was a miracle he ever came into the arena to watch me practice or to see any of my games. On his really bad days, he wore shades in the arena. One of the guys had made fun of him once, but when I knocked his ass down on the ice for it, he didn't make that mistake again.

I set my gym bag down and gently shook Sterling's shoulder. He groaned and swatted at me, making me chuckle. God, he was so fucking adorable. "Sterling, come on. Practice is over," I told him.

He slowly cracked open one eye. "It's already that late?" he muttered.

I nodded. "Come on. Get up. Let's go for a drive."

He slowly sat up and stretched before standing to his feet. I picked up my bag, and Sterling grabbed my other hand in his, linking our fingers together. "How did therapy go?" I asked him.

He shrugged. "It was therapy." That was Sterling's code for: it wasn't miserable but it sucked. "I told her about my flashback, and we kind of worked through part of it. I'm also trying a new med." He blew out a soft breath, his hand tightening around me. "I asked for it this time."

I knew how bad it had to be if Sterling willingly asked to try another medication. And I hated that I couldn't take away all the horror that had happened to him and make it my own. I hated it with a fucking passion because I couldn't *stand* the knowledge that my boyfriend was suffering.

Trauma was a fucking bitch. And I wished the man who did this to him was dead. I wished it with every fiber of my being.

"I hope it works," I told him.

He nodded, staring at the ground. "Me, too, Graham."

Sterling ended up falling asleep in the passenger seat on the way to the cliffs. When it was warm, it was normally a make-out spot for a lot of couples—and hookups—but now that the weather was cold, it was empty. Which was just what Sterling needed.

"Why are we stopping?" Sterling groaned, lifting his head from the window.

He blinked at the view in front of us before his breath slowly left him. "Wow," he breathed. He quickly pushed open the door faster than I thought his half-asleep self could do and got out, closing it behind him. I scrambled to follow him. "Graham, this is... I don't have words."

I shoved my hands in the pockets of my hoodie when a breeze blew. I could smell the salt from the ocean right below. The waves were crashing against the rock wall in repetitive, soothing motions, and across the water, the rest of the city we lived in was visible. The lights lit up the sky in a beautiful array of colors.

I took a seat on the edge of the cliff and let my legs dangle over, letting Sterling decide if he wanted to follow. Sterling quickly sat beside me and grabbed my hand in his, linking our fingers together. I gently squeezed his hand in mine. "Thank you for bringing me here. It's just what I needed."

"I know," I told him softly. I cupped his cheek and turned his head to face me. Slowly, I leaned forward, giving him the opportunity to back away. I didn't know where he was in his headspace, so I made sure to tread carefully. But when he closed the remaining distance between us and expertly moved his mouth against mine, I knew exactly where he was at.

Our tongues danced together in a slow, erotic dance. My body came alive, and it felt like sparks were igniting all over my skin as we slowly made out, savoring each other and this moment and the absolute peace surrounding us.

The safety we felt with each other.

"I love you," I rasped once we parted to catch our breaths. Our chests were heaving, and I was so hard it hurt, but none of that mattered in this moment. I needed Sterling to know I was madly in love with him. That he was my one. "The moment I laid eyes on you freshman year, my entire fucking life changed. I've loved you from the moment you told me you don't like to be touched. I love you so goddamn much that I ache when you're not within reaching distance." I slid my fingers into his hair and rested our foreheads together, closing my eyes. "You are my beginning and my end, Sterling, and I cannot exist without you."

Sterling crushed his mouth to mine and pushed me back on the ground, crawling over me so he was straddling my hips. His hands roamed all over my body, and I did the same to him, licking and nipping at his lips. Our kiss was sloppy and filled with passion, and it warmed every single part of me as if I was lying on a beach in Florida in the hot, summer sun.

"I love you, too," Sterling finally managed to get out between kisses. "So goddamn much, I could never put it into words. You're my safety net. The reason I'm able to crawl out of bed every morning, even on my bad days. You're the reason I didn't leave school and go home my first month of college." He leaned up on his elbows to look down at me. "You're just *my reason*, Graham."

I cupped his cheek. "I'll always be your reason, baby."

He leaned down and kissed me. And I proceeded to have the hottest make-out experience of my fucking life.

7

Graham

I drove with one hand on the steering wheel, the other on Sterling's lap, our fingers linked together. We'd spent hours at the cliff, and it was well past midnight now. The only reason we left was because the temperature kept steadily dropping, and my hoodie wasn't thick enough to rival the temps. Well... and my stomach was rumbling, which Sterling proceeded to call a parasite.

"How's your appetite?" I asked Sterling as we neared campus.

"Eh," he muttered. "Not very good."

I headed for the store closest to us that was open twenty-four hours. "So, it's a soup and crackers night?" I asked him.

He rolled his head to the side to look at me, a small smile tilting his lips. "That would be preferred."

I nodded. "Then that's what we'll get for you."

Sterling hummed, his tired eyes shutting for a moment before he forced them to reopen. "You're too good to me."

I shook my head and hit my indicator to turn into the parking lot of the supercenter. "Baby, you deserve everything good and kind in this world, and you're not getting damn near enough of it."

He squeezed my hand in response, and that was okay because I didn't need anything verbal from him. I just needed him to know how I felt. His feelings always came through his actions, and I couldn't believe how blind I'd been to them before.

But I wouldn't make that mistake again because I didn't want to miss another fucking thing about Sterling Hardison. My eyes had been closed long enough.

Now, they were wide open.

"Do you think I'll ever be normal?" Sterling surprised me by asking as we lay together in my bed. We were on our sides facing each other, our heads on one pillow. He'd been silently running his fingers over my body for the past hour with only the sound of the movie playing breaking the silence. Not wanting to get in the way of his wandering hands, I'd been resting my hand on his bare thigh, brushing my thumb back and forth over his hair-roughened skin.

I frowned at Sterling. "Normal is overrated," I told him honestly, shivering when he hit a certain sensitive spot on my side. "I mean, what the fuck even is normal? Everyone has got some kind of demon in their closet or something else hindering them from being what someone might deem normal." I pecked his lips, and the corners of his quirked up into a smile. "I love you just as you are, Sterling. What's normal for you, right now, is the only kind of normal I want."

He sighed. "Sometimes, I wonder what it might be like to be able to touch a stranger without having a panic attack. Or just be able to get hard without trauma forcing me to go soft again."

I frowned at him. "I think those things will go away with time, especially the ED," I assured him. "Maybe one day, you and Dr. Clancy will find a medication that works for you to allow that part of your life to be what's medically normal. And if your touch phobia never disappears, then that's okay, too, Sterling."

He slid closer to me, our bodies pressing together. My dick was reacting to his closeness, but I ignored it. "You think I could survive in normal society like that?" Vulnerability laced his words, making my chest ache.

I rested my forehead against his and pressed a kiss to his lips again. "I think you can do whatever you put your mind to, baby." And I meant that. Sterling was incredible. He'd survived something so traumatic, it might've killed someone else.

He slid his palm over my heart. "How do you always know what to say?"

I chuckled. "I'm just speaking my mind, Sterling."

He hummed and leaned forward, smoothing his lips over mine. I wound my arm around his waist and pulled him closer, deepening the kiss. He moaned into my mouth and parted his lips. Groaning, I rolled him onto his back, deepening the kiss as I went.

I couldn't get enough of him. I was so fucking addicted to Sterling. And there was no cure for me, not that I wanted one.

I wanted to spend the rest of my life high on him.

For the first night in a while, Sterling didn't have any nightmares or flashbacks. His Xanax put him right out once he remembered to take it, and he slept so hard, he slept through his first two classes of the day. I probably should have woken him up, but I couldn't bring myself to. He *needed* the sleep after the rough night he had the night before.

And because I was a lazy fuck, I stayed in bed with him. I probably should have taken a shower and rubbed one out, but I couldn't bring myself to move. Hence why my dick was poking him in the back. Wasn't much I could do about it when I was only wearing a thin pair of boxers.

Sterling groaned and stretched, his ass rubbing against my cock, and I moaned low in my throat, shutting my eyes for a moment. Then, Sterling decided to be a little tease and purposely rubbed his perky ass over my shaft. I clamped a hand on his hip, stilling his movements.

"You're playing a dangerous game," I rasped.

He rolled over to face me, and he trailed his fingers over my dick through my boxers. I shivered, my breath hitching in my throat. "We're already obviously late for classes."

"So late," I groaned. "Please stop fucking teasing me, Sterling."

A wicked grin slid across his lips, and then he disappeared beneath the blanket, pulling my cock out of my boxers. "Sterling, what are you—*oh, fuck*," I moaned when the hot, wet suction of his mouth wrapped around my shaft. He bobbed his head and swallowed me to the back of his throat. A shout ripped from my lips as my hips strained off the bed. "*Oh, God,*" I hissed. "Please don't stop, baby. That's perfect. Feels so good."

He swirled his tongue around my shaft before swallowing me back down. I whimpered, my fingers lacing in his hair. When he didn't freak out, I began to thrust up into his hot, tight throat, whimpers and moans falling from my lips. He felt so damn good. I didn't want to know why he was fucking expert level with this, but I'd definitely reap the fucking benefits.

"I'm so close," I panted. The base of my spine was tingling, and my balls were drawing up tight against my body. "I'm going to come, Sterling," I tried warning him in case he didn't want me to spill down his throat.

He just moaned around me and sucked me deeper. That moan shot straight to my balls, and I shouted his name, spurting my cum down the back of his throat. I felt him swallowing around me and almost wept at the pure bliss of it.

He slowly made his way back up my body, a little smirk playing on his lips. "How was that for a good morning?"

I growled and rolled him to his back, looming over him. "Fucking perfect," I rumbled. Then, I settled my body on top of his and proceeded to kiss the fucking daylights out of him.

I grunted in shock when Sterling moved the curtain aside and stepped into the shower stall with me. Then, a smirk curved my lips. That was until I ran my eyes over his body. Little scars littered his upper thighs, white against his peach-colored skin tone. I swallowed thickly and forced myself not to focus on them, instead drinking his strong but lean form, honed from years of constantly running when life got to be too much.

His cock was soft but long, and if he was a grower when he got hard, then God fucking help me. I was going to be praying to Him while Sterling rocked my world.

"Surprised you're in here with me," I murmured, reaching out to draw him under the water with me. I'd gotten a shower after practice, but my muscles were burning from the grueling practice I'd just endured, and I needed more hot water to soothe the ache.

"You looked exhausted. Wanted to check on you, and I needed a shower," Sterling informed me with a shrug.

I walked my fingers down his spine. He shivered in response, stepping closer to me. I bit back a moan at how good his damp skin felt against mine. "I'm okay," I assured him. "With our first game of the season being Saturday, Coach is pushing us extra hard this week."

"Let me bathe, and I'll give you a massage in our room. Just got to find the massage oil."

I chuckled as Sterling poured shampoo into his palms. "Did you even bring it back with you for this year?" Sterling used to give me massages after hard practices or rough games last year since he was finally comfortable with touching me and me touching him. And fuck, his massages were the best. Apparently, because he wanted to help me, he'd watched a ton of YouTube videos to learn the best way to soothe my muscles.

Even before he became my boyfriend, he was the best fucking guy on the planet. I didn't know what I'd done to deserve him, but I would forever cherish him.

Sterling nodded and began to scrub his scalp, lathering the shampoo. "It's probably stuffed into the depths of one of my desk drawers."

I waited under the steaming hot water, watching as he rinsed his hair and washed the hard planes of his body. I was hard from watching him and jealous of the water running over his tight body, but I wasn't particularly in the mood to do anything sexual. I was too fucking tired. I really just wanted to sprawl out in bed and fall asleep to the feeling of Sterling massaging my tense muscles.

Once we were back in the room, I walked over to my closet while Sterling went searching through his desk drawers for his massage oil. I grabbed the jersey I'd ordered a few weeks ago for Sterling and closed my closet back, turning to face him. I'd ordered it so he had something special to wear to my games to kind of name him as my biggest fan since we were best friends, but now I wanted to give it to him to wear to my game on Saturday as my boyfriend.

I cleared my throat, and Sterling glanced over his shoulder at me before standing up straight, turning his whole body now to give me his attention. I stepped forward and held the jersey out to him. It was folded in just a way that it displayed my last name on top. He took it from me, so many questions in his gaze as his eyes roamed over my face.

"I want you to wear that," I rasped, emotion thickening my voice. "On Saturday, I mean. And every game after that. I want you to wear it as my boyfriend. Please." I was stumbling, showing how nervous I clearly was, but Sterling didn't bat an eye.

He unfolded it, a grin spreading on his lips as he ran his eyes over the front before flipping around to the back, my last name and number proudly displayed. He set it on his desk and then grasped my hips, pulling me to him. When his lips met mine, the nerves running through me quieted, and I sank into his embrace, eagerly kissing him back.

"Of course, I'll wear it as your boyfriend," he told me once we parted, both of us breathing a little heavier. "I'd be honored to, Graham."

"Good," I rumbled, squeezing him to me. "I don't know why I was so nervous to ask."

He chuckled and kissed my jaw. "You get nervous over the weirdest things, babe."

My heart skipped a beat in my chest at the pet name. I'd been using them, but this was Sterling's first time. And fuck, it rocked my world.

"Babe?" I croaked. "You've never called me anything but my name before. Well, unless you're being an ass."

He chuckled and turned back to his desk. "I can be an ass," he teased.

I snickered. "Babe is just fine," I told him. I shouldn't have made a big deal out of it, but I couldn't help myself. I was all warm and fuzzy inside from it.

"Got it!" he suddenly cheered, pulling out the bottle of massage oil. He turned to me, proudly holding it up. "Strip out of those sweats, baby." He practically purred the word at me, and I shivered, quickly moving to do what he'd ordered. When he called me those sweet names, I would do anything in the fucking world for him. "And get on the bed on your stomach. I've got magic to work."

I moved onto the bed and laid on my stomach, turning my head to the side and draping my arms by my sides, though I moved them away from my hips a bit so Sterling had room to settle on my ass. Once he was comfortable, he began to move his slick hands over my tense back, and I moaned, my eyes sliding shut.

"That is magic," I groaned.

Sterling just quietly laughed.

8

Graham

The past couple of weeks with Sterling as my boyfriend had been almost pure bliss. He'd come to my first game of the season wearing my jersey and every game after that, even the away games. Most afternoons, he sat in the stands of the arena and did homework while I busted my ass during practice. His nightmares were now few and far between with his medication, and he hadn't had one in the past three nights, which was a record.

I hated that having an actual flashback

had been what pushed him into trying a new medication, but I was also kind of thankful for it. Because Sterling couldn't keep living like he had been. It would've worn him down too quickly, no matter how hard he fought. And I couldn't keep watching him dig himself deeper and deeper into his misery.

The entire campus now knew Sterling and I were together, which helped to kill the ED rumors, and come to find out, we'd had an entire group of people "shipping" us the entire time we'd been friends, and our ship name was Sterham. Kind of weird, but it was cute, too. Someone had even created an entire Instagram page dedicated to us and took random pictures of us and posted them.

I was guilty of saving every single one of them to my phone.

"Why is everyone so insane around Halloween?" Sterling grumbled as he ducked beneath a ghost hanging from the ceiling on our hall. I'd been smart enough to walk around it.

Most of the doors on our hall were

decorated for the upcoming holiday, and some of the students had taken time to even decorate the hallway. Hell, even our bathroom looked like Halloween threw up in it. But I had to admit, I was excited. Halloween parties were always pretty fucking epic, and I was hoping that now that Sterling was on Xanax, he might be open to going to the party with me this year.

"Because Halloween is like the best holiday of the year," I told him in a duh tone. "Parties are fucking epic. There's candy galore. And the girls are hot as fuck."

Sterling rolled his eyes at me. "We're not inviting a girl into our bed, Graham." I would never, but it was still funny. All I needed was Sterling. The girls were just hot as fuck to look at now.

I chuckled and opened our dorm room door—one of the only ones on the hall not decorated, much to both mine and Mrs. Hardison's dismay. Sterling had put his foot down on "not contributing to the craziness", as he put it.

My hands spanned his waist once our

dorm room door was shut behind us and tugged him closer to me. "I enjoy looking, baby, but you're the only person I want in my bed," I rasped before claiming his lips in a sweet kiss. He sank into my hold, his arms winding around my shoulders. The kiss wasn't heated or passionate. It was intimate, saying everything we didn't say with our words.

Regardless, I felt his cock pressing against me, and I moaned, struggling to rein in my lust. That was another big change—Sterling was actually getting hard lately. We'd been touching more, and every day, his erection lasted longer and longer. He was getting excited about the prospect of finally getting to have sex, but I could also see he was trying to not get his hopes up about it.

I forced myself to pull back from him. Licking my lips, I ran my eyes over his face, drinking in every beautiful thing about him. "Will you come to a Halloween party with me? The team is throwing it."

Sterling frowned at me. "I don't like parties, Graham."

I groaned and let my head fall back on my shoulders overdramatically before I looked back down at him. "I know you don't, but you're my boyfriend, and I *really* want you there. I want to dance with you and watch dumb, drunk idiots do stupid shit together."

He sighed, but I could see the amusement he was trying to hide in his eyes. "If I agree, then when I want to leave, we leave. No questions asked. No begging to stay. And you know I can't drink with my med."

I grinned. "Babe, I never drink. Why do you think I always came back from parties sober? Alcohol gives me a pounding headache after only a couple of sips." I shook my head. "Can't stand it."

He grunted and stepped back from me, reaching down to adjust his cock. I licked my lips as I unashamedly watched him. A teasing smile tilted his lips, and he winked at me. "Fine. I'll go with you. But I'm *not* dressing up."

I snorted. "I know better than to push for more," I assured him. I grinned at him, so happy he'd agreed. "But I *will* be dressing up."

Sterling rolled his eyes and settled on my bed, which had basically become ours. We hadn't slept apart since getting together. And if I had my way, we'd never sleep apart again... unless I had an out-of-town game. But even lately, I'd been managing to sneak him into the hotel room with me if the game was far.

"I wouldn't expect anything less, Graham."

I just quietly laughed because when he saw my outfit, I knew he'd have a hard damn time keeping his hands to himself. And that was my hope. I wanted to give him everything he wanted, and I knew how badly he wanted to have sex. And selfishly, I wanted it just as badly.

Because I *really* wanted Sterling to top me.

I eyed myself in the mirror, a smirk pulling at my lips. The black, leather pants

I was wearing clung to my legs like a second skin and outlined the shape of my cock perfectly. My chest was bare, and I'd slicked oil over my skin to make my abs and muscles shiny, which I knew would drive Sterling fucking crazy. Big platform boots were on my feet, and they went all the way up to my knees, an insane amount of buckles holding them closed. In my hand was the piece that completed my outfit: the Ghostface mask.

"Are you—*holy fuck*," Sterling choked out as he walked into our room from the bathroom. He'd gone to wash his face since I was hogging the mirror in our room, and I'd taken advantage of his absence to change into my outfit for the night.

I turned to face him, a cocky grin pulling at my lips. "You like?"

Sterling groaned, his jeans pulled tight over his hips due to his erection. "Fuck, you look good," he rasped.

I waggled my brows at him. "We've got time if you want to play," I teased.

Sterling chuckled, but his smile was strained as he continued roving his dark eyes over me. "I want to see how long this manages to last me," he said, waving down in the direction of his dick—which was still hard. Hope was stirring in my chest. "Come on. Let's go see what you like so much about all this fucking insanity."

I grabbed his hand in mine and slid my Ghostface mask over my head before walking with him out of our dorm room, locking it behind us. Normally, Sterling and I were about the same height, but with these boots, I was taller than him, and I had to admit, I kind of liked it.

"Those boots are almost as hot as the way your pants make your ass look," Sterling said as we made our way down the stairs.

I laughed. "I'll keep that in mind."

The party was already in full swing when we arrived, and it was already packed. I had to park a street over to even get a parking spot.

"This better be worth it," Sterling

muttered as he eyed all the cars we passed. "Because I didn't expect to have to walk."

I snorted. Oh, the fucking hypocrisy. "Are you really complaining about walking when you literally walk everywhere you can to avoid driving?" I teased.

He cut me that side-eye look that told me he was annoyed with me. I snickered and squeezed his hand in mine. "That's because I *want* to walk to those places. I thought since we were driving, we wouldn't have to walk."

Dropping his hand, I wrapped an arm around his shoulders and tugged him close against my side. Pressing a kiss to his temple, I said, "Babe, stop trying to find reasons to hate tonight and just trust me."

He sighed, sinking against my side. My heart fluttered in my chest. Pretty sure at this point, the damn organ was growing wings. "I do trust you, Graham. More than I trust anyone else in the world."

"Good. Then believe me when I say that tonight will be fun."

He just huffed but didn't say anything else, which told me he was going to give me a chance to prove him wrong. And I would. I was determined to. I was hoping I could make this night memorable for us both.

Bass was thumping through the speakers strategically placed around the house when we walked in, and it was so loud that it rattled my teeth and thumped through my chest. Numerous people, some I didn't even know, greeted me as we made our way through the crowded house. Sterling stuck close to my side as I weaved us through the partiers to the makeshift dance floor in the living room.

Popularity could suck sometimes, especially when all I wanted to do was spend time with Sterling.

All the couches and chairs had been pushed against the wall to make room for dancers, and couples—or probably more like hookups—were already making out. Some of them were in partial states of undress.

Sterling grimaced, but before he could even try voicing to leave, I turned his back to me and gripped his hips, moving our bodies to the beat of the song. It didn't take him long to fall into rhythm with me. A moan crawled up my throat when he started grinding his ass against my thick shaft. The fingertips of my left hand dug into his hips, and with my other hand, I slipped my hand around to the front of his jeans and cupped him.

He was hard, almost threatening to burst through his zipper. Moving my hand, I gripped his hair and tugged his head to the side, trailing the end of my mask along his neck. His breath stuttered out of his lungs on a shaky exhale, and I faintly heard him groan my name as our hips continued moving together.

Suddenly, he turned to face me, his cheeks flushed. His dark eyes were bright as they locked on mine. "Take me upstairs," he growled in my ear.

I sure as fuck did not have to be told twice. Grabbing his hand in mine, I linked our fingers together and tugged him off the dance floor, heading for the stairs near the front door. We raced up them, passing multiple other people making out, and I was pretty sure one of them had said fuck finding a room and decided to screw against the wall on the staircase.

I pushed open a door and breathed a sigh of relief when I saw it was empty. Quickly, I tugged Sterling inside before slamming the door shut behind us and flipping the lock so we wouldn't be disturbed.

"I need these off," Sterling growled, undoing the ties on my leather pants. As soon as they were loose, he tugged them down my legs. Once they stopped at my boots, Sterling crouched and began unbuckling my boots. I quickly stepped out of them and then yanked my pants off with my socks. My Ghostface mask was tossed across the room. I didn't even care where it landed. I just needed my boyfriend on that bed.

"Get undressed," I commanded as I sat on the edge of the mattress. I fumbled in the nightstand drawer, pulling out a bottle of lotion. It wasn't lube, but it would do. I wasn't new to anal sex, and I was bottoming tonight. I wanted Sterling to have the experience of sinking into a tight, warm ass.

And I wanted the experience of feeling

him inside of me. I'd been imagining it since freshman year.

Sterling tugged his shirt over his head, and I laid back on the mattress, spreading my thighs. After squirting lotion onto my fingers, I reached between my cheeks and rubbed my finger around my hole. Sterling groaned, his eyes locked on my hand as he hurried to unsnap his jeans.

"I want to bottom," I rasped as I sank a finger inside. I moaned, gritting my teeth. Fuck, that felt good. I hadn't bottomed in a while, and I forgot how good it felt to have something inside of me like this.

Sterling tugged his jeans and boxers down his legs and shoved his sneakers off. Once he was completely naked, he prowled toward the bed. I inserted a second finger, and my back bowed off the bed.

"Take them out," Sterling ordered. I quickly did as he said and watched as he lubed his fingers up with lotion before gently sinking them inside of me. I kept my eyes locked on his, my chest heaving as Sterling slowly scissored me open.

"You're so gorgeous," I murmured, my

chest tightening. I was so fucking happy and grateful that I got to be his first. It meant the fucking world to me.

"You're everything," he rasped, sinking a third finger inside of me. I moaned his name, my eyes shutting for a moment in bliss before I forced them back open. His other hand was working his cock, slicking it up with a shit ton of lotion. He was long, thick, and hard, and I couldn't wait to feel him inside of me.

I'd even gotten tested when we started dating just to make sure I was clean. Coach made us get tested every month, but I wanted to be extra cautious. Because Sterling deserved that courtesy.

"Fuck, that feels good," I groaned as he worked his fingers in and out of me. "I need to feel you inside of me, baby. I'm ready. I swear, I'm ready."

Sterling swallowed thickly, his Adam's apple bobbing. He suddenly looked nervous, and I didn't fucking like it. "If I go soft—"

"I don't care," I told him fiercely. "I want you however much I can have you, Sterling.

That's all that's fucking mattered to me. That's all that's *ever* mattered."

He blew out a soft breath and nodded his head. I scooted back on the mattress, and he crawled onto the bed between my thighs, his shaft bobbing with each movement. Reaching out, I ran my fingers over him, and he moaned, his eyelids fluttering as he struggled to keep his gaze locked on mine.

"If I manage to stay hard," he chuckled, "I may not last long."

I shook my head. "Still don't care, babe."

He drew in a deep breath and batted my hand away, making me chuckle. He wrapped his hand around the base of his cock before pressing against me. I bore down, and he slipped inside. He moaned, his head falling forward as he slowly inched inside of me. He was thick, and it burned, but *fuck* it burned so good. I never wanted to feel anything else ever again.

"Oh, God, Graham," he groaned as he sank further and further inside. "I can't—you feel too fucking good."

I leaned up on my elbows and brushed my mouth to his. His tongue flicked out and licked across the seam of my lips. I opened for him immediately, and he dove inside, tongue-fucking my mouth as he began to screw up inside of me. Falling back onto the mattress, I tugged him with me. My legs were hooked over his arms, and he bent me nearly in half as he began to screw up inside of me.

"Yes, yes, yes," I chanted between hot, heavy kisses. "Sterling, that feels so good," I moaned. "So fucking good. *God*," I groaned.

"Not gonna last," he panted.

I reached between us and began to stroke myself, whimpering each time he pegged my prostate. "Come inside of me," I begged. "I *need* you to come inside of me, Sterling."

He shouted my name, his hips stuttering. When I felt his warmth begin to fill me up, I cried out his name, my neck arching as my cum spurted between us. Sterling landed on top of me, his face tucked into my neck, and a moment later, I felt his hot tears running down my skin.

Quickly, I rolled us to the side and wrapped him up in my arms before throwing a leg over his hip. "I'm here," I whispered, clutching him to me.

"I..." His voice trailed off, but I knew what he was trying to put into words.

After *years* of never being able to keep an erection, not only had he been able to stay hard long enough to have sex, but he also hadn't had any kind of flashback, hadn't heard *his* voice, and he'd actually been able to participate in the act of sex.

That was a huge, monumental thing for him.

I ran my fingers through his hair and pressed a kiss to his forehead, my own tears burning in my eyes. For him. Because being able to experience this with him meant the fucking world to me.

"I know, baby," I rasped. I tucked his head under my chin. "*I know.*"

9

Graham

It took a few minutes for Sterling to get himself together, and the entire time, I just held him, doing my best to hold him together while he got out some of his emotions. Crying was cathartic, and Lord knew he was overdue for a good cry, especially after so long of holding himself together.

"I think I'm ready to head back to the dorm," Sterling quietly said, pulling back from me a little. His eyes were bloodshot, and his face was damp from his tears.

Reaching up, I gently thumbed away some of his tears, my eyes running over his face.

"Then we'll head back," I quietly told him. "Let's wash your face, clean up a little, and then we'll head to the car."

He nodded and leaned forward, pressing a kiss to my lips. I sighed and ran my hand down his arm, smiling softly at him once we parted. He easily returned the smile, and it reached his eyes, letting me know he was okay despite the high emotions running through his body. As long as he was okay, we could work through everything else together.

Once we'd cleaned up a bit and Sterling had splashed some cold water on his face to alleviate some of the redness, we quickly got dressed. He grabbed my hand in his, and I opened the door to the room before leading him down the stairs. The party was even more packed and wilder than it'd been when we came upstairs, so Sterling stuck close to my back, somehow managing to avoid being touched by anyone else.

It was something only someone with a major touch phobia could accomplish, honestly. Even after knowing him for a little over two years, it still astounded me how easily he did it.

Once we were outside, Sterling breathed a sigh of relief, and his hand loosened around mine, though he didn't release it. We were quiet as we made our way down the sidewalk to the tiny side street we ended up parking on. When we reached my car, Sterling leaned back against the passenger side and grasped my hips, pulling me to him so our bodies were flush.

"Thank you for tonight," he murmured. He pressed a kiss to my jaw, and I shivered, my fingers sliding along his sides. "I needed that."

I gripped his chin and angled his head up a little so I could lean down and kiss him. "If you're up for more tonight, we can try it," I told him.

He appeared to be thinking for a moment, and so I just busied myself with lightly touching him over his layers of clothes, waiting for him to give me a response. I was beginning to shiver, the heat of the party officially leaving me, but I would endure it until I had his answer.

"I'm not sure if I'll be able to bottom," he warned me, "but I'd like to try."

My heart stuttered in my chest for a moment at the thought of him trusting me enough to do that. I cupped his cheek and kissed him again, trying to hide how much his request had moved me. "We stop as soon as you say the word," I promised. "I don't care if I have to be the bottom for the rest of our lives, Sterling. Besides," I shrugged, "I like being the bottom." I shot him a cheeky grin.

He snorted and gently shoved me away. "Get in the car. You're shivering."

I winked at him as a particularly rough one shuddered through my body, making my teeth chatter. "It's just the effect you have on me, babe."

He barked out a laugh and opened the passenger door, sliding into the seat.

When we got back to our dorm room,

Sterling immediately backed me up against the door, his mouth hot against mine. I groaned and slipped my fingers under his t-shirt, pulling the fabric over his head. As soon as his mouth was back on mine, I mapped the planes of his flat stomach, traced his ribcage, and moved up to gently rub my thumb over his nipples.

He hissed a breath through his teeth, and I grinned into our kiss before lightly pulling on them. He ground his cock against mine, a moan spilling from his mouth. Kissing him harder, I began walking him backward to my bed, and when the back of his legs hit the mattress, I tumbled him down onto it, our teeth clashing for a moment before we moved back into our fluid rhythm.

"Get the lube because I'm not waiting once I'm naked," Sterling rasped.

I kissed him hard before reaching over into my bedside table for my bottle of lube. Once I had my hand on it, I tossed it onto the mattress and then moved back over Sterling, grinding our hard lengths together as we continued making out. His feet pressed into the mattress, his shoes having gone missing at some point, and he pushed up against me as I pushed down on him.

"Off," Sterling snarled as he pushed at my leather pants. I quickly stood and unbuckled my boots before kicking them off and peeling off my leather pants. Sterling shoved at his jeans, and once he was naked, he beckoned me back down.

Our lips met in a fiery clash, and we both moaned at the feeling of our bodies coming together. I blindly reached for the bottle of lube, and once I had it, I slicked my fingers up before reaching between our bodies for his hole.

He tensed when I found it, and I immediately stopped, leaning back from him. When I began to move my hand away, he grabbed my wrist, shaking his head at me. "I need to see you. That's all," he whispered.

"Okay, baby," I soothed, my heart clenching in my chest at the nervous look on his face. "Just remember, you're in control here."

He swallowed thickly and nodded. I circled my finger around his hole, and he kept his hand locked around my wrist. Our eyes never disconnected as I slowly eased a finger inside of him.

He moaned, his legs spreading wider as I breached him. "Oh, f-fuck," he whimpered, a breath shuddering from his lungs, making his chest shake a little. "That feels so good."

"It's going to feel even better when I'm inside of you," I promised.

He licked his dry lips as I worked my finger in and out of him, and when I added a second, a groan sounded from deep within his chest. He began fucking himself on my fingers, his breaths already panting from his lungs. His cock was leaking all over his stomach, the tip red and angry.

He looked so fucking beautiful like this. So needy and perfect.

"One more," I rasped, warning him because I knew it would burn.

I inserted a third finger and went in search of his prostate. As soon as I found it, he cried out, spurting cum all over his flat stomach. I grinned and continued working him open. With my other hand, I swiped some of his cum up and popped a finger into my mouth, moaning at the taste of him.

"Oh, that's hot," he groaned, his heavy-lidded gaze hot on mine.

A wicked grin tilted my lips. Easing my fingers out of him, I got my knees under me better and began to lube up my cock. Sterling watched me with hungry eyes. As I moved forward, I grabbed his hand and linked our fingers together.

"You're safe," I promised him.

He nodded his head. "I know," he rasped.

I pushed against him, and after a moment of resistance, I slid inside him and past that first, tight ring of muscle. He shuddered and moaned, his other hand gripping my thigh. I pumped my hips in small strokes, easing further and further inside of him until my balls were flush against him.

He was so hot and tight. Felt so fucking

good around me. I'd never felt anything better.

"*Fuuuuuck*," Sterling moaned, voicing my exact thoughts. His dick was already filling back up, and he reached down to begin stroking it. I moaned at the sight. He was perfect. So fucking perfect. "Please move. *Fuck*, Graham, I need you to *move*."

Immediately, I began to ease in and out of him. I didn't want this to be rough and quick. I wanted to take my time with him. Savor him. Make love to him. Make sure that safety net in his mind never slipped because I didn't want to do a damn thing that would rip him out of this beautiful moment we were sharing.

"Graham, oh, *God*, please don't stop, baby. *Please*," he begged.

Fuck, he was so pretty when he begged me like this. It was officially one of my new favorite things.

"I won't," I managed to get out through gritted teeth. He was so tight and slick and fuck, I didn't think I was going to last. But I'd somehow make it until he came again. Some fucking how. I was determined.

He began to stroke faster while I kept my hips at the same speed. He was writhing on the bed beneath me, his curls a damp mess on his head. His dark eyes were hazy as he watched me.

A moment later, his back arched, and he shouted my name, his third orgasm of the night washing through him. Snarling, I spilled inside of him, choking out his name right before my vision momentarily went white from the force my orgasm wrenched itself from my body.

Not wanting to crush him with my dead weight, I eased out and flopped to the side, dragging him into my arms. Our breaths were choppy, our chests heaving. Sweat glistened on our skin, and his cum smeared all over my abs and chest as we clung to each other.

"I didn't know it could feel like that," Sterling panted.

"With me, I'll make sure it *always* feels like that," I promised, pressing a kiss to his damp forehead. He tasted like salt and everything Sterling. I couldn't get enough of it.

He pressed a kiss to my sweaty throat. "We need showers, but I don't know if I can move."

A breathy laugh spilled past my lips. "Yeah, me neither."

After a few minutes, our breathing was regulated once again, and his cum was drying on our bodies. He was also beginning to get uncomfortable with my cum spilling out of his ass.

"Shower," he muttered as he slid out of bed. He grabbed his jeans off the floor and tugged them on commando before shoving his feet into his shower shoes.

I groaned, not wanting to move, but I wasn't ready to be away from him yet. "Hold on, and I'll join you." Slipping off the bed, I grabbed a pair of dirty sweats from the floor and yanked them on. Sterling was impatiently waiting on me by the door by the time I finally got my towel, toiletries, and a clean pair of boxers together.

"Come on," I told him, opening the door for him. We quickly made our way down the hall and into the same shower stall. After stripping, I started the water and dove beneath it. I snorted out a laugh when Sterling shoved me out of the way and stood beneath it, letting the water pressure wash the cum off his body.

"I officially hate the feeling of cum on my skin," Sterling muttered.

I hummed. "Should we use condoms?"

The look he shot me told me no, we should not, and I was stupid for even suggesting so. I snickered and stepped under the water with him, tugging him into my arms. "Sex is always going to be messy then," I warned him.

He waved his hand around, and a smile tilted his kiss-swollen lips. "Guess I'll be taking frequent showers."

I arched a brow at him, a teasing smile playing on my lips. "Frequent?"

He grinned at me and flicked his tongue out over my lips. If I had enough energy, I would've backed him up and gotten him hard again before sucking him to the back of my throat, but I was practically dead on my feet.

"Yeah—frequent. Think you can keep up with that?"

I laced my fingers in his hair and yanked his head back, licking a path up his neck. He swallowed back a moan, though a tiny bit of it slipped out. "Is that a challenge?" I murmured.

He just smirked at me.

Game on, baby.

"I am so fucking hungry," Sterling groaned as he cut into his pancakes. I rolled my lips into my mouth to hide my laughter... and to keep my smart-ass remark to myself.

Sterling narrowed his eyes at me. "I know that look," he said, pointing his fork at me. "Go on. Spit it out, Graham."

"It's just... Well, after last night, I bet you are hungry." The dirty look he sent me had me laughing so loud, the older couple at the table next to us shot me a dirty look. I just gave her a little finger wave and turned back to face Sterling. He was shoving pancakes into his mouth and studiously ignoring me. "Oh, come on, babe," I groaned. "You walked right into that one."

"Shut up," he mumbled around a mouthful of food.

His phone suddenly lit up with the picture of his mom requesting a FaceTime call before I could tease him more. Immediately, he set his fork down and grabbed his earbuds, passing me one before he stuck his in his ear. Once we both had ours in, he answered her call and propped his phone up on the napkin dispenser so she could see both of us.

"Good morning, my beautiful, handsome boys!" Mrs. Hardison exclaimed. "Ooh, are those pancakes? Honey, I want pancakes for breakfast!" she called out to her husband.

I laughed. "Good morning, Mrs. Hardison," I greeted. She was always a pleasant little hurricane. Sterling shoved more pancakes into his mouth, waving at her. "To what do we owe the pleasure?" I teased.

"Trish and I have been talking, and we're thinking of doing Thanksgiving at your house this year as a big family," Mrs.

Hardison informed us, but she was looking at me. "This way, we can be prepared for family holidays and already have a routine in place for when you two get married."

Sterling choked but managed to get what he'd swallowed back up before I could move to help him. He gulped down some water as I quietly laughed. I wanted to be like Mrs. Hardison when I got older—absolutely no filter. Just say whatever the hell came to mind. And endlessly tease my kid.

"Mom," Sterling choked out, "can you *not*? Christ, we just started dating."

She waved him off. "We both know Graham's going to marry you, hun." Sterling's cheeks colored. Instead of responding, he just focused on his pancakes. I grinned. Anyway, she wasn't wrong. I had plans to make Sterling mine in every way I could. "Anyway, I just wanted to call and tell you both to prepare to go to Trish's for Thanksgiving. We'll make it a quick affair because I know you have to be back on campus for hockey, right, Graham?"

I nodded. "We have a game that Saturday, so Coach is letting us have Wednesday and Thursday off, but he's expecting us to be at practice at three on Friday."

"Good!" she exclaimed. "Then you can show up Wednesday, and we can have some quality family time. I'll let you two finish your breakfast. Sterling, honey, I'm so happy to see you with a good meal in front of you."

Sterling smiled at her. She blew him a kiss before ending the call. Sterling arched a brow at me. "My mom is going to steamroll over Mrs. Hurley."

I shrugged. "My mom loves your mom, so I don't think we need to worry about any steamrolling. For two people with so much money, your parents are the most down-to-earth people we've ever known—aside from you," I added. Sterling waved me off, letting me know adding that part hadn't been necessary because he wasn't offended. "My mom considers them coming into our lives as a blessing."

Sterling snickered. "Don't ever let Mom hear you say that. She'll burst into tears and be a mess for all of Thanksgiving.

Making a difference in someone's life is all my mom strives to do."

I chuckled. "Noted."

Sterling twined our legs together under the table and tucked back into his pancakes. My heart was fluttering in my chest, ready to explode with how happy and in love with him I was.

"I love you," I blurted.

Sterling smiled at me. "I know. I love you, too, babe. Now let me eat please."

I laughed and tucked back into my own food, letting comfortable silence settle between us.

10

Sterling

Graham parked my car alongside the curb in front of his mom's house. We'd considered driving his car since he was more comfortable with it and we both knew I wasn't going to drive, but he needed an oil change and a new tire on his car since the tread on one of his was pretty low. I'd already texted Mom about it as soon as he mentioned it this morning, so I knew by the time we got back to campus, both things would be taken care of for him.

She was always taking care of little

things like that for him so he could focus on school. Whenever he told her she didn't need to, she just came back with, "Well, it's on my insurance, and I'd rather my rate not go up if you have an accident so I can spend extra money on margaritas on the weekends." And he'd shut right up.

The front door opened, and both of our moms rushed out of the house. I laughed and quickly got out, shutting the door behind me. Mom catapulted herself into my arms, and I quickly caught her, squeezing her to me.

She cupped my cheeks when I set her on her feet. "Oh, my boy, you are positively *glowing!*" she squealed. She hugged me again, pressing a kiss to my cheek. I didn't even need a mirror to know she'd left red lipstick on my skin. It was her signature color. If it wasn't a blood-red shade, it was the wrong color. "I'm so glad you're happy," she told me.

I smiled at her and pressed a kiss to her cheek. "I missed you, Mom."

She squeezed my cheeks together before releasing me and rushing at

Graham. Mrs. Hurley smiled at me but didn't come near me. I was comfortable with both her and Mr. Hurley, but I still didn't feel safe enough with them to allow touching. And thankfully, neither of them had ever been offended by that. They just nodded, welcomed me into their home, and respected the boundaries I had clearly laid out for them.

It was easy to see why Graham was so amazing. His parents had raised him well. Raised him into a kind and compassionate young man who cared about others and empathized deeply.

"Your father ordered pizza," Mom told me as she ushered us toward the house. Graham reached out and grabbed my hand, and both of our moms beamed at us as if we were the greatest things on Earth. "It's a chill-out night since we're doing so much cooking and eating tomorrow."

"We?" I teased.

Mom waved me off. "Don't you dare come near that kitchen, Sterling."

I snickered. I was hopeless in the kitchen, despite my mother's numerous efforts to teach me how to cook. I got distracted too easily and also had a bad habit of never hearing the timer. I did the same thing with microwaved food. The timer would go off, but by the time I remembered I needed to eat, it was cold and I had to reheat it again. It was a never-ending cycle.

Dad nodded at me when we walked into the house. "Come get some food, boys. We're just getting ready to watch the hockey game we missed watching last weekend."

Since Graham and I had become roomies freshman year, Dad had made it a point to watch every single game in support of Graham. And then he and Mr. Hurley would get together and talk about it. It was kind of awesome how well our families got along even before we started dating. It was like the universe's way of saying we belonged together.

And damn if that didn't make me feel all warm and fuzzy inside.

I took a seat on the couch, and Graham sat beside me. Dad handed us a plate of pizza each. Graham's had three slices and mine had one. "I wasn't sure how your appetite was after the drive," Dad explained as if I might be upset that he gave Graham more.

I waved him off. "This is great, Dad. Thanks. If I want more, I can get it."

Graham and I were shoulder to shoulder, eating pizza. His eyes were focused on his game, and every once in a while, he would comment about where he messed up or another teammate did. Dad and Mr. Hurley were adding things, too, and suggesting tips to improve.

I just relaxed back into my seat and enjoyed my pizza since I'd already seen the game and had done my fair share of yelling until my throat hurt. It took me a good twenty-four hours for my throat to recover.

My cheeks colored through when the camera panned to me wearing Graham's jersey. Mom happened to be coming into the living room, and she shrieked when she saw it. "You two are so adorable!" she exclaimed. She pressed a kiss to the top of both of our heads. "You make my romantic heart so happy," she gushed.

Graham grinned at me, feeding off my mom's praise of us. "You do look adorable in my jersey, babe."

I rolled my eyes at him, but my stomach erupted in butterflies at his words.

I liked that I looked good in his jersey. All his little groupies could kindly fuck off now.

I quietly opened the bathroom door in the hallway, being careful not to alert any of our parents that we were in the bathroom together. I mean, we were sharing a bed, but being naked in the shower together was harder to explain away.

I could see Graham on the other side of the clear shower curtain, his cock in his hand as he slowly stroked himself. Mine plumped in my sweats, and I stepped in, quietly shutting the door back behind me. Graham's eyes were closed, no doubt picturing me as he got off. It was something he'd confided in me during a stupid game of twenty truths we'd been playing a couple of weeks ago when the power went out on campus during a particularly bad storm.

I dropped my sweats to the floor and tiptoed to the shower curtain, slowly peeling it back and stepping into the tub. Graham still had his eyes closed, and he groaned, squeezing the base of his shaft.

Quickly, I gripped his shoulders and pressed the front of his body against the wall. "Sterling, what the—*oh fuck yes*," he hissed when I slipped two fingers inside of him. He was still slick from when we'd had sex before making the drive here, and my fingers easily sank inside. When he moaned, I shoved two fingers of my other hand into his mouth, gagging him. His cock pulsed precum, and his tongue swirled around my fingers.

"Bend over just a little," I whispered.

He immediately moved into position, and I gripped my shaft, pressing against his hole. He bore down, and I sank inside, gritting my teeth and holding my breath so I wouldn't make a sound and alert our parents that we were currently fucking in the shower. Getting caught would be *so* embarrassing.

He resumed stroking himself as I quickly worked my cock in and out of him. We didn't have time to linger, not if we didn't want one of our moms coming to bang on the door and shout about hot water. And man, my mom having to take a cold shower? The house would become a war zone.

Having grown up poor, my mom couldn't stand being uncomfortable. Too hot? Too cold? Clothes not fitting right? She couldn't stand it. It was one of the reasons she had been so accommodating when it came to my trauma. She understood.

Graham gagged on my fingers when I shoved them further down his throat, and I grinned manically, quickening my pace to chase my orgasm. He bit down on my fingers when he came, and I sank my teeth into his shoulder as I spilled inside of him so I wouldn't make a sound.

"Fuck," Graham panted when I dropped my fingers from his mouth. Gripping his hips, I gently eased out of him, watching as my cum immediately ran down his thighs. "That was hot."

I chuckled. "If you're done, I need to quickly shower before my mom comes up here to embarrass us."

Graham snorted and grasped the side of my neck, pulling me into a tender kiss. "I'll see you in bed, babe."

He stepped out of the shower and began drying off. Somehow, I managed to rip my eyes off his toned, strong physique and lather shampoo into my hair. I was done in about three minutes and quickly got out, drying off and wrapping a towel around my waist since I forgot to bring clean clothes with me.

"Sterling," Mom whisper-shouted when I stepped out of the bathroom. I flinched and quickly stepped back from her, my heart hammering against my breastbone at not only being frightened by her sudden appearance but also because she had used that voice on me. She didn't move though—just stayed where she was. "You can't just walk around someone else's house with only a towel, hun."

"Just need to get dressed," I mumbled, trying to swallow down the panic attack that was looming over my head.

Her face suddenly softened, and she backed up two steps, giving me even more space. I quickly rushed into Graham's room and sank back against the door, swallowing thickly to get rid of the icky feeling in my throat. My heart was racing to the point it hurt. All she'd done was say my name in that scolding manner, but I'd already felt too vulnerable by being out in the open like that without clothes, and it'd nearly sent me over the edge.

Graham was suddenly cupping my face in his hands, his eyes boring into mine. "Breathe, Sterling," he gently commanded. He stroked his thumbs over my cheeks. "Just breathe. You're safe. I'm here."

I wrapped my trembling arms around him and clutched him to me, releasing a shaky breath. He combed his fingers through my hair before slowly leading me to bed. We tumbled down together, the towel coming loose. But he just tugged the blanket over us and continued holding me.

"Just stay here with me," he coaxed. "It'll pass."

I nodded and burrowed even further against him, my heart rate calming. When the trembling ceased, I flopped onto my back and blew out a harsh breath. "I forgot clothes, and then Mom said my name in that mom way that moms have," Graham chuckled, "and I kind of freaked out."

Graham ran his hand over my chest. "You're safe here," he promised me, continuously saying those words because he knew I needed it. "You want to get dressed?"

I nodded and slid off the bed, prowling to my bag we'd brought in earlier. Once I was dressed in a pair of sweats and a long-sleeve shirt, I crawled back into bed next to Graham. Immediately, he wrapped his arms around me and rested his chin on the top of my head. "Don't go to sleep without taking your medicine," he warned me.

"Took it before the shower," I quietly

informed him. "Now hush and let me sleep."

Graham laughed softly and pressed a kiss to the top of my head. The soothing, rhythmic stroking of his hand down my spine lulled me to sleep.

Where no monsters could touch me anymore. Instead, my dreams were always filled with Graham.

Because with him, I was always safe.

There was so much food. I had no idea why mom went all out like this every single year, but this year, she'd managed to outdo herself. Every kind of food you could imagine for a Thanksgiving dinner was placed on the counters and the stove and lined up on the kitchen table, too.

"Mom," I groaned, staring at all the food. "This is *a lot*."

"You and Graham can take some back to campus with you," Mrs. Hurley told me, speaking for her. "Besides, I know my son, and he's going to eat as much as he can."

Well, I couldn't argue with that.

"Your son's stomach is a parasite."

Mrs. Hurley laughed, her shoulders shaking. "That's the best way I've heard anyone describe Graham's eating habits," she snickered. "Honey, you hear that?" she called to her husband. "Graham's stomach is a parasite."

His booming laughter filled the house. Graham stepped into the kitchen, and his mouth dropped open just as the parasite in question began to rumble with hunger. "Oh, this looks *good*," he groaned. "Can we eat? I'm starving."

Mom laughed. "Help yourself, hun," she told him, handing him a plate. She handed me one too, and I grabbed a little bit of stuffing, a little bit of turkey and gravy, some mashed potatoes, green bean casserole, and a roll. My boyfriend, however, grabbed one of everything, even going as far as getting a second plate to continue heaping food.

"I don't know where you put it all," I told him once we were settled on the floor of the living room with the coffee table in front of us.

He rolled his eyes at me. "I'm a growing boy, Sterling."

I snorted. "All of that is going to catch up with you when you're old."

He winked at me. "As long as you continue to love me, I don't care."

I sighed. "I could never stop loving you, Graham," his eyes got all melty on me, "but I will hound you about your health," I warned him.

He waved me off. "I can put up with anything as long as you love me," he reiterated. "And speaking of love," he began digging in his pockets, making me frown at him. Finally, he held up a small ring. It was black with a multi-colored band splitting it. A soft smile tilted his lips. "I'm not asking you marry me yet because I've got goals to reach before then, but I am making you a promise."

My eyes welled with tears. Mom had both of her hands over her mouth to hold in her squeal, jumping up and down. Mrs. Hurley was smiling at us. I stared back at

Graham, my throat working as I tried to swallow down my tears.

"I love you, Sterling. I love you with every fiber of my being. I want to always be your home. Your safety. I want to always continue being your reason for the rest of our lives. By giving you this ring, I'm promising to always be yours. To be the support you need. To give you a bright future and always be a safe place for you to land when life gets overwhelming."

He drew in a deep breath, his own eyes shimmering with tears, his hand shaking. "So, will you please accept this ring as a symbol of my promise to you?"

Immediately, I nodded. "Yes," I rasped. "A hundred times fucking yes, Graham."

He slid the ring on my finger and then kissed me. Mom finally screamed, and I smiled against my boyfriend's lips. His stomach rumbled again, completely ruining the mood, and I laughed.

He rested our foreheads together, his eyes bright with happiness. "I love you, Sterling."

"I love you, too, Graham." I patted his

stomach. I roughly cleared my throat, not wanting to burst into tears in front of our parents. "Now eat before that thing starts eating you."

Dad barked out a laugh from his position on the couch.

EPILOGUE

Graham

I leaned forward, bracing my elbows on my knees as I watched my teammates skate around the ice, doing their best to break the tie with the other team. Going pro had been a dream come true for me, though it didn't come without its frustrations—like not being able to start the game. Coach wouldn't give me the damn opportunity to prove myself. I understood he had more "experienced" guys he could put on the ice, but I knew what I was doing.

And apparently, the ones on the ice couldn't get their shit together today. This should've been an easy game, but we were struggling.

Turning, I glanced at the stands, spotting my boyfriend watching with his arms crossed over his chest, his jaw clenched. He was close to the box I was sitting in, so I'd heard him cussing and yelling more than enough to know he was pissed about this, too. He'd even yelled at my coach to get his head out of his ass and put me in the game.

I'd gotten a dirty look for that one as if I'd somehow put Sterling up to it, but I had just brushed it off. Coach would come to learn one day that my man wasn't one to be fucked with—not when it came to this sport and me being able to play.

Another thing—Sterling was my manager. He didn't have to deal with people unexpectedly touching him because there was no reason for anyone to get that close to him. And it also meant we were together all the time. His safety net never went anywhere. He was doing so much better than he had been in college, but he still had his moments, and we were finding new triggers all the time. But he worked through them with Dr. Clancy, who was still his therapist, only they did their sessions virtually now.

A player hit the ice, his head bouncing off of it, and his leg was bent at an awkward angle, making me wince. The entire arena went silent as everyone waited for the verdict from the medics, who rushed onto the ice. I rose to my feet to get a better view of what was going on. After a minute, it was determined he needed a hospital. He was conscious, but he more than likely had a concussion, and his knee was snapped out of place.

For his sake, I hoped it wasn't a career-ending injury. It was my biggest fear—getting an injury that ended my career. I lived and breathed hockey, and I wasn't sure how I'd survive without it.

"Hurley!" Coach barked. I looked over at him. "You're in."

After a quick huddle with my team, we

made our way onto the ice. Sterling was cheering for me, and I grinned at him before placing my hand over my heart and then pointing my finger at him. He grinned and blew me a kiss.

It had taken my teammates a minute to get used to the fact that I was bisexual, but they eventually came around. They supported me, and they even helped when it came to my online presence and the assholes who liked to come sideways at me and Sterling.

I got into position, and when the puck slid in my direction, I quickly took off like a shot, swiping it from the other team and swiftly making my way across the ice, dodging the other team's players left and right. Once I was close enough, I shot it into the net, officially breaking the tie between our teams and putting us in the lead.

I chanced a quick glance at Sterling and chuckled at how rambunctious he was being. My good luck charm never let me down.

I raised two fingers to my helmet, right

over my lips, and then raised them up at Sterling. The camera panned to me as I did it, and then it shot to Sterling, who did the same in return. Hearts exploded over the screen, and I chuckled.

The rest of the game went smoothly and without a hitch, just like I knew it would. As soon as it ended, my teammates were all over me, shouting their congratulations in my ears. I laughed, soaking it all in and congratulating them on a job well done, too.

As soon as I had space, I searched for Sterling in the roaring crowds, and when my eyes landed on him, I placed my hand over my heart, then to my helmet where my lips were, and held my fingers out to him. When he began to return the gesture, I dropped to one knee. His jaw dropped open, his eyes almost bugging out of his head. My teammates started shouting, their excitement for us tangible in the air.

But this was sort of the moment I'd been waiting for, though I couldn't carry the ring I'd bought him around while I had games. It was sitting safely in our apartment back in Seattle in my sock drawer.

"Will you marry me?" I mouthed at him.

"Yes!" he shouted, his voice barely carrying to me over on the rink. But the fact that it had showed how loudly he'd yelled his answer.

I grinned and did our thing again, and this time, he returned it, his cheeks pink, his eyes bright.

God, I loved this man so fucking much.

Sterling was all over me as soon as we walked in the door of our hotel room. He licked into my mouth, his fingers tangled in my damp hair. I moaned and kicked our door shut before pressing him against it, my hands tearing at his clothes. Sex with us was always wild and frantic at first. We couldn't ever seem to slow down until after we'd gotten our first orgasm out of the way.

"Fuck, I can't believe you got playing time today," Sterling panted as he yanked my hoodie over my head. "You were so fucking hot on that ice. I love watching you play."

I yanked his jeans down his legs as he kicked out of his shoes. "I can't believe you fucking agreed to marry me," I growled before I kissed him again. Our tongues tangled together, and I rutted against him, slamming his body harder against the door. He moaned, which was practically a beg to continue being rough.

"Better believe it," he rasped as I picked him up. He wound his legs around my waist as I carried him over to the bed, dropping down on the mattress with him sitting astride my lap. He gripped my hair and yanked my head back, trailing his lips down my throat. "I expect my ring when we get home."

"Oh, you'll get it," I promised. "And you better fucking wear it everywhere. I want everyone to know who you belong to." I wiggled out of my boxers and slid back on the bed, tugging him with me. "You're *mine*."

"Always," he panted as he pulled a plug

out of his ass, shooting me a cheeky grin. I growled and flipped him over onto his stomach before rising up behind him. I *loved* how he always prepped for me. I'd do the same if landing on a butt plug when I hit the ice didn't hurt so fucking much. Did it once. Sure as fuck would never do it again.

"You ready for me?" I rasped, one hand on his spine to keep him with me. When he couldn't see me, he still needed constant contact, which was where my hand came in. And fuck, I was always more than willing to touch him.

"Yes," he pleaded. "Fuck me, Graham. Fuck your fiancé."

Oh, fuck yes.

I quickly sank inside of him, and he moaned my name. Reaching back, he gripped both of his ass cheeks and spread himself apart. I snarled and began fucking him, my hips audibly snapping against his ass with every stroke into his ass.

"Yes," he groaned. "Don't stop, Graham. That feels so fucking good. Please, God, don't stop."

"You going to come untouched for me?" I managed to heave out between labored breaths. My body was sore from the game, but I would suffer through anything to be with Sterling. But shit, I was going to feel this tomorrow.

"If you keep fucking me like this, then yeah. Definitely," he moaned.

"You feel so good," I panted. "So good, baby. I'm close. Please, fuck, tell me you're close, too."

"I am," Sterling groaned. "*F-F-fuuuuck*," he cried out as he came all over the bedsheets. I gritted my teeth and spilled into him, marking him as mine from the inside out for the umpteenth time this week.

I just couldn't fucking get enough of him.

I dropped to my back beside him as he collapsed onto his stomach, both of us trying to catch our breaths. His fingers linked through mine, and I gave his hand a gentle squeeze.

"How was it fucking your fiancé for the first time?" he breathlessly asked.

I chuckled. "So fucking good. And once I catch my breath, you can have your go at it in the shower."

He groaned, his eyes shutting. "Sounds like a plan."

I rolled onto my side and tugged him into my sore arms for after-sex cuddles. Our legs tangled together immediately, and he burrowed against me like he was trying to crawl into my skin. His sigh fanned across my bare, sweaty skin, making me shiver.

"I love you," he murmured. "Thank you for continuing to be my reason."

"I love you, too," I whispered, pressing a kiss to the top of his head. "Thank you for letting me continue to be your safety."

He snuggled even closer and wound his arm over my waist, his other hand pressing to my chest, right over my heart. My eyes slid closed.

The shower would have to wait. With Sterling in my arms like this, I just wanted to sleep.

Before I even realized it, I was out like a light, only mumbling a tiny complaint when Sterling pressed a kiss to my lips and slipped out of bed to go shower and get the cum off his skin.

Want more of Sterling and Graham?
https://dl.bookfunnel.com/hwlbld1q37

ALSO BY WEST GREENE

Want to stay up-to-date with sales, new releases, new preorders, etc?

Join my newsletter!

https://westgreenebooks.com

Facebook

Instagram

Facebook Group

Twitter

Patreon

Pinterest

Access my merch store here.

ABOUT THE AUTHOR

West Greene is a romance author that specializes in short, steamy books and erotic shorts.

All your instalove needs can be found in one of her books, whether you're looking for possessive men, men with no morals, spicy FF romance, a boy just needing his Daddy, a twink just needing love, or even the other woman to get her HEA.

West Greene refuses to be stuck in one trope or type of romance. She loves variety, and she's definitely going to share that variety with her readers.

Printed in Great Britain
by Amazon